Rachel was pregnant!

She was crying and laughing—there were so many things for her to consider now. She was going to have a baby, for heaven's sake—Ross's baby!

Suddenly, out of nowhere, some spoilsport part of herself held up a red light. *Hold it, Rachel,* it said. *Have you lost your mind? How can you be so thrilled about this baby when you might not have a husband for much longer…?*

But what if Ross was right? What if he had really changed for good this time? Did she dare take the chance that he had?

She really wanted to. And it wasn't just for the sake of the kids…or the child she carried….

Dear Reader,

Take one married mom, add a surprise night of passion with her almost ex-husband, and what do you get? *Welcome Home, Daddy!* In Kristin Morgan's wonderful Romance, Rachel and Ross Murdock are now blessed with a baby on the way—and a second chance at marriage. That means Ross has only nine months to show his wife he's a FABULOUS FATHER!

Now take an any-minute-mom-to-be whose baby decides to make an appearance while she's snowbound at her handsome boss's cabin. What do you get? *An Unexpected Delivery* by Laurie Paige—a BUNDLES OF JOY book that will bring a big smile.

When one of THE BAKER BROOD hires a sexy detective to find her missing brother, she never expects to find herself walking down the aisle in Carla Cassidy's *An Impromptu Proposal.*

What's a single daddy to do when he falls for a woman with no memory? What if she's another man's wife—or another child's mother? Find out in Carol Grace's *The Rancher and the Lost Bride.*

Lynn Bulock's *And Mommy Makes Three* tells the tale of a little boy who wants a mom—and finds one in the "Story Lady" at the local library. Problem is, Dad isn't looking for a new Mrs.!

In Elizabeth Krueger's *Family Mine,* a very eligible bachelor returns to town, prepared to make an honest woman out of a single mother—but she has other ideas for him....

Finally, take six irresistible, emotional love stories by six terrific authors—and what do you get? Silhouette Romance—every month!

Enjoy every last one,

Melissa Senate
Senior Editor

Please address questions and book requests to:
Silhouette Reader Service
U.S.: 3010 Walden Ave., P.O. Box 1325, Buffalo, NY 14269
Canadian: P.O. Box 609, Fort Erie, Ont. L2A 5X3

WELCOME HOME, DADDY!

Kristin Morgan

Silhouette
ROMANCE™
Published by Silhouette Books
America's Publisher of Contemporary Romance

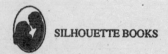

SILHOUETTE BOOKS

ISBN 0-373-19150-2

WELCOME HOME, DADDY!

Copyright © 1996 by Barbara Lantier Veillon

This edition published by arrangement with Harlequin Books S.A.

® and TM are trademarks of Harlequin Books S.A., used under license.
Trademarks indicated with ® are registered in the United States Patent
and Trademark Office, the Canadian Trade Marks Office and in other
countries.

Printed in U.S.A.

Books by Kristin Morgan

Silhouette Romance

Love Child #787
First Comes Baby #845
Who's That Baby? #929
Rebel Dad #982
A Bride To Be #1055
Make Room for Baby #1084
Welcome Home, Daddy! #1150

KRISTIN MORGAN

lives in Lafayette, Louisiana, the very heart of Acadiana, where the French language of her ancestors is still spoken fluently by her parents and grandparents. Happily married to her high school sweetheart, she has three children. She and her husband have traveled all over the South, as well as other areas of the United States and Mexico, and they both count themselves lucky that their favorite city, New Orleans, is only two hours away from Lafayette.

In addition to her writing, she enjoys cooking and preparing authentic Cajun foods for her family with recipes passed on to her through the generations. Her hobbies include reading—of course!—flower gardening and fishing. She loves walking in the rain, newborn babies, all kinds of music, chocolate desserts and love stories with happy endings. A true romantic at heart, she believes all things are possible with love.

Fabulous Fathers

Hi, guys,

It's me—your dad. Listen up, okay, 'cause I've got something real important to say.

You see, I was a big jerk in the past, and I hurt you and your momma. I can't undo my mistakes, but I want both of you to know how truly sorry I am. I realize now that the three of you are the most important people in the world to me, and I want us all back living together again as a family. It's my dream, and I know that it's yours, too.

So, I have this plan, see, to make our dream come true. Now I know you don't understand all this adult stuff I'm trying to explain, but the truth is, I hurt your momma real bad—and…well…you see, unfortunately, adults aren't always as forgiving as kids are. It's going to take me a bit more time to win back her trust. But I want you to know that, no matter what, I'm not going to give up until I do. One day real soon, we'll be a family again. I promise.

In the meantime, I want you to remember that I love you and your momma more than anything in the whole world.…

Love always,

Daddy

Chapter One

Ross Murdock could hardly believe the sick, lonesome feeling that had settled in his gut only seconds ago.

Needing a moment to himself, he eased his way through the jubilant crowd of well-wishers and climbed the wide, winding staircase to the second-story balcony of one of Houston's ritziest hotels. He stopped at the top of the staircase and stared down below where the birthday celebration in his honor was now in full swing. Inhaling deeply, he canvassed the ballroom quickly, allowing his attention to linger momentarily on the four-piece jazz band located at the back of the room. With a mild degree of consideration he noted that several couples had been unable to resist its lively beat and were dancing.

Just beyond the bandstand was a glass wall that rose to the vaulted ceiling several floors above him. From his elevated viewpoint Ross could see that several other guests had wandered outdoors and were now standing near the pool.

Inside the ballroom was a long line of narrow tables draped in white linen and decorated with huge bouquets of fresh, fragrant flowers; doily-lined trays of hors d'oeuvres and elegant-looking desserts were placed in strategic groupings between the centerpieces. Champagne—Ross's favorite, he knew—flowed freely from a huge silver fountain at the center of the room. A well-stocked bar in another corner offered a wide variety of other cocktails.

It seemed that tonight's celebration was turning out to be quite an event. Undoubtedly the newspaper and national magazine reporters who were sifting discreetly through the crowd, looking for a good story, would write in tomorrow's society headlines that the invitation-only guest list for Ross Murdock's thirty-fifth birthday bash included celebrities and government officials from across the country, as well as many of Houston's most elite citizens.

Ross knew that he should've been thrilled. In spite of his initial objections to having a birthday party given in his honor, several of his closest friends had gone through a great deal of trouble and expense in planning tonight's gala event. And, the truth of the matter was, as recent as a few minutes ago, he'd been having the time of his life.

What the hell had happened to him? The need to be alone had struck him full-force and he'd wandered up the stairs for a few quiet moments to himself.

Frowning, Ross quickly gulped down the last swallow from his glass of champagne and heard rather than listened to the sounds of idle conversations and periodic outbursts of laughter that drifted up to him.

Sinking deeper into his own private thoughts, he leaned against a thick white support column that, like the glass wall behind the bandstand, rose several stories above him. For a moment he was unaware of the direction his thoughts had taken. Finally, though, he realized that he'd been mentally calculating his many ups and downs during his illustrious ten-year career as one of the world's top investment specialists.

Undoubtedly his friends and business allies alike, most of whom were here at the party, would have accused him of nitpicking by bothering to count his losses. After all, this was his thirty-fifth birthday and not too many men his age could claim to be a self-made multimillionaire. He was, without question, the man of the hour. The man everyone said had the Midas touch.

And he'd been lucky. Damned lucky. His losses over the years had been few. In fact, he could sum up an accurate assessment of his brilliant career by saying that he'd suffered only one major catastrophe and that was...

Well, actually, his one big loss had nothing to do with business. In truth, it was personal. It was, in fact, the reason he'd come to his own birthday celebration alone.

Not that he couldn't have had a date, if he had wanted one, Ross quickly reminded himself. He knew plenty of women who would've jumped at an invitation from him. He just hadn't bothered with asking anyone, although, for one fleeting moment a couple of days ago he'd considered asking his estranged wife Rachel to attend the party with him. But then, at the last minute before dialing her telephone number, he'd decided not to make the call. After all, it wasn't easy for a man like him to crawl. Not even to the woman he loved.

Besides, Rachel would never have accepted his invitation, even if he had been successful in ignoring his pride long enough to ask her. It had been six months now since she, his once-upon-a-time, loving wife, had so gallantly walked out on him in spite of his protests, taking their two young sons, Jorgie and Danny, back to their hometown in south Louisiana.

For the most part, she had her life now and he had his. Their kids were their only connection. Rachel had insisted on it being that way. And in the end he had gone along with her wishes, thinking that eventually they would sit down together and work out a plan toward solving their marital problems. Unfortunately, that wasn't happening. Rachel was still shutting him out. In truth, he didn't know what to think anymore. In fact, she was now talking about a possible divorce, and, of course, he was shouting a loud *no way*. But even his futile protests weren't enough to convince her that he still cared. Something had to give—and soon.

Not that he didn't honestly deserve the treatment he was getting from Rachel, because he knew he did. Still and all, he'd learned his lesson. So why, then, couldn't she recognize that and give him another chance?

Damn her, anyway.

His problem was, he loved her too much. In fact, sometimes he almost felt as though he had no more control over his life because of it—which, for him, was quite an admission in itself. According to his many business associates, Ross Murdock was always in control of the moment. And yet, one small but determined woman had turned his life into chaos. Somehow, it didn't quite seem fair that it had been so easy an accomplishment for her.

And yet, even as Ross stood there, trying to erect a steel wall around his memories of Rachel, one of those memories in particular was bold enough to knife its way through his metal guard, giving him a sweet, poignant image of her clothed in the white lace wedding gown that she'd worn as his bride. He remembered how her silky blond hair had fallen in soft waves over her slender shoulders, and how her light blue eyes had shone with an everlasting love that he had thought would never dim...

And, God, but even today, even after all the hurt and pain and misunderstandings that now separated them, both physically and emotionally, it seemed her simple, fragile loveliness could still take his breath away—though, in truth, it had been her inner beauty that had actually stolen his heart so long ago. On the day that she'd walked out on their marriage, he had called her a silly little fool for leaving without even giving him a second chance. She'd called him a workaholic, a man who had become possessed by greed and power. She'd said he'd become a stranger to her and the kids—and that his neglect of their emotional needs told her that he didn't need them in his life any longer. He'd tried telling her that he was only working to secure a sound financial future for them. But Rachel had had her mind made up and had walked out anyway. Just like that.

"Ross?"

The sound of his name startled Ross from his thoughts and he whirled around to see that his good friend and attorney, Christian Chandler, had climbed the winding staircase and was standing only a few feet away. "Yeah?"

Christian pulled his light brown eyebrows together in a frown. "Are you all right?"

Ross mimicked the same expression. "Yeah—sure. I, uh, I just needed a moment to myself, that's all."

"Look, I'm sorry for interrupting," Christian replied, "but I was told to find you. There's an emergency telephone call for you in the main foyer."

Ross's frown deepened. "For me?" he exclaimed.

Christian nodded. "I'm told it's Rachel."

Ross's heart thumped hard three times and then leapt into his throat. "Good grief, Christian, why didn't you say so to begin with?"

Ross immediately started down the wide staircase. His friend followed on his heels.

The last emergency telephone call he'd gotten from Rachel—or rather, on her behalf—was when she had suffered the miscarriage of their third child at the end of last year while he was away in Canada on a business trip. In fact, something had happened to her on that night while she'd lain recovering in her hospital bed. Something so drastic that it had somehow affected her entire way of thinking toward him—their marriage—their whole way of life. It was after that night that he'd no longer been able to reach her.

It took only seconds for Ross to reach the telephone, but, already, a thousand thoughts were racing through his mind—none of which were slowing the gallons of adrenaline that had begun mainlining into his bloodstream. All the while he was trying to convince himself that maybe all Rachel wanted to do was to wish him a happy birthday. And yet, deep down inside, he knew better. Besides, he'd already gotten the card she'd sent him. Therefore, her calling him here, tonight, at a birthday party she had no part in giving him, had to mean but one thing. She had an emergency of some kind.

Dammit all, Ross thought to himself, how in the hell was he supposed to take care of his family when Rachel had herself and the boys residing in another state? She had no right to be doing this to him. Okay, so maybe he hadn't been the best husband and father in the world, but he damned sure hadn't been the absolute worst, either. And somehow, sooner or later, he was going to have to find a way to make her see that.

Overanxious now to hear Rachel's voice, Ross picked up the receiver and pressed the flashing button on the telephone. His guts were in knots. "This is Ross Murdock."

"Oh, Ross..."

It *was* Rachel, and she was crying—which in itself, without another single word from her, was enough to gut him wide open. In fact, it stopped his heart in midbeat. An image of her tear-streaked face flashed across his mind.

"My God, Rachel, what's wrong?"

"It's Danny," she sobbed. "H—he's missing."

Ross's heart was pounding, hammering against his breastbone. "What do you mean, he's missing?"

"I—I've looked everywhere and I can't find him. A friend of his from the neighborhood is missing, too. When I last saw them, they were playing together."

The sheer terror in her voice for the children's safety knifed its way across the miles to slash him deeply. His own sudden fear seemed to constrict his air passages, and breathing became an effort.

"Have you called the police?"

She began to sob harder. "Y-yes. They're searching, but they can't find them, either." And then between her tears she added, "Oh, Ross, I'm frantic that something terrible has happened to them."

"Okay, just calm down, Rachel, and tell me how long they've been gone."

"Since after lunch. Around two o'clock."

Ross glanced at his Rolex watch. It was eight o'clock at night. Damn. Already his five-year-old son had been missing for more than six hours. *Six hours.* That was a long time for a little kid to be lost. It would be dark outside soon. Where could he be? Were he and the other kid together? Were they all right? The thought that something might have happened to them made Ross feel even sicker. If he had been there. . . . "Why didn't you call me sooner?"

Her cries were low as she spoke into the receiver. "Be-because I thought we would've found them by now. I—I still can't believe this is happening. He's such a sweet little boy . . . Oh, God—I should've been watching him more closely."

Ross sucked in another deep, steadying breath. As much as he sometimes wanted to literally throttle Rachel for the disruption her leaving him had caused in their lives, now wasn't one of those times. In fact, his compassion for her in that moment was overwhelming. "Look, take it easy, Rachel. It's only been a few hours. The police are going to find him."

"I know," she replied, and Ross could imagine her shaking her head like she always did when she was upset over something and was trying to make herself feel better. "I keep telling myself that."

"Then keep on telling yourself that—and don't worry. They'll find him, okay?"

Once again Ross filled his lungs with air, only this time he released it with a harsh sigh. Be real, Murdock, he told himself. At the moment there was no way that either he or Rachel could take such well-intended advice. Not as long as Danny was missing. Still, saying the words to Rachel in the hopes that she might somehow find comfort in them was worth a try. Even if she only listened enough to stop crying. It was pure hell for him to hear her sobbing like that. "Where's Jorgie?"

As she spoke, her breathing came in jerky spasms. "He's right here, sitting with me at the kitchen table. He's pretty upset."

"Yeah, I can imagine," Ross sympathized. "Look, tell him I'm on my way, okay?"

"Ross, please, hurry," Rachel pleaded in an anxious voice.

"I'm leaving now," he replied.

"Okay," Rachel mumbled, and Ross knew it was taking every ounce of courage she possessed to control her emotions. A moment later the line clicked dead.

One thing about Rachel, she might have convinced herself she didn't need Ross in her world anymore, but when it came down to their two children, he knew that Jorgie and Danny were her world.

But in truth, until this very moment, he hadn't honestly given much thought to just how important his kids were to his world, too. He'd pretty much taken their existence for granted.

Well, now he wouldn't ever again have to worry about finding the answers to those kinds of questions, because the expanding void in the pit of his stomach was telling him all he needed to know about their importance in his life. In truth, Rachel and his kids were his world. Heaven help them all, but it was time that he made her see that.

Ross immediately dialed the number to the hangar where his twin-engine airplane was kept and ordered it ready for immediate takeoff. Then he turned to Christian, who waited nearby. "I've got to get out of here without drawing attention."

"What's wrong?"

"Danny's missing," Ross replied, and his gut knotted even tighter.

His friend paled. "My God..." Then he quickly surveyed the room. "Look, I remember seeing an employee elevator at the other end of this corridor. Take it and it'll probably take you down to house-keeping. In the meantime, I'll go out front and send a cab around to pick you up in the rear."

"Good idea," Ross replied, immediately heading in the direction that his friend had indicated.

"What happened?" Christian asked, following in step right behind Ross.

"I don't know all the details, yet—only what Rachel could tell me through her tears. But it seems that Danny and a friend of his were playing in Rachel's backyard and then just vanished."

"Kidnapped?" Christian asked in a grave tone of voice.

"That's what I thought at first. But then, the other kid's missing, too. Maybe they just wandered off." Ross shook his head. "I don't know, maybe that's just wishful thinking on my part. But either way, it's all my fault."

"Look, man, you can't blame yourself for this."

Ross paused only a couple of seconds and then said, "Yeah, well, if I had been a decent husband to Rachel, she wouldn't have left me, and Danny would be safe right now."

"You don't know that for sure."

"I damned sure do," Ross said meaningfully. "And I tell you something else, once Danny is found and this crisis is behind us, I'm going to do whatever it takes to make Rachel see that I need her."

One corner of Christian's mouth lifted in a fleeting smile. "That's the best news I've heard from you in a long time." He clapped his hand down on Ross's shoulder. "Hurry out of here and find your son."

Just then the small employee elevator at the end of the corridor opened and Ross stepped inside.

"Let me know about Danny," Christian said.

"I will," Ross replied as the elevator doors slid shut.

By the time Ross slipped out the back entrance to the hotel, he had to wait only a moment before a yellow cab swerved around the corner to pick him up.

He handed the taxi driver two one-hundred dollar bills and gave him directions to the airport. "Make it fast, buddy," Ross said. "My son's life is on the line."

And in that moment Ross knew in his heart that all his millions of dollars could never buy him the love that Rachel and his kids had once given to him so freely. He had been such a fool to take that love for granted.

Rachel sat at her kitchen table and stared aimlessly into space. In truth, she didn't know how much more of this nightmare she could take without falling completely apart. She had thought that the worst two days of her life—the day she'd miscarried their little girl, and the day she'd walked out on Ross—were behind her. But she'd been wrong. Today, her youngest son was missing, and no one seemed to be able to find him. She was living through a parent's worst nightmare come true. Surely, Ross would be arriving soon. Somehow, in spite of her own warnings to the contrary, she needed him here with her.

When Danny and his friend Orlan had first turned up missing, she and Orlan's mother had tried for an hour to find them on their own before finally realizing they needed additional help. Since then, the police had taken over the search, and Rachel, like Mindy, had promised to stay put in her house and place the responsibility of finding the two children in their capable hands. Only her son and his friend were still missing, and it had been nearly eight hours now.

This was all her fault, Rachel thought. Danny was her responsibility. He depended on her to take good care of him, and she'd let him down. She would never forgive herself if something happened to him. In truth, she wouldn't blame Ross if he was furious with her for losing their son.

There was a knock on the back door that led inside to her kitchen where she, Jorgie and her sister Jan sat at the table waiting anxiously for the latest update sent back to them every so often from the search party roaming the neighborhood and surrounding area for any sign of the two small boys. Their efforts had become hampered by the onset of nightfall, now more than an hour old. Still, Rachel's hopes that her son and his friend would be found at any moment raged on. Therefore, every time she heard a knock at her back door, her heart fell into her stomach. *Maybe this time the news would be good.*

Jan was the first to jump to her feet. "I'll get it," she said, hurrying in that direction. Her younger sister had been at her side practically from the start of this ordeal. Ever since Rachel had called her with the disturbing news that Danny and his friend were missing. In truth, Rachel guessed that she had needed someone, after all. Someone who wasn't a complete basket case like herself and was capable of seeing to it that Jorgie didn't somehow wander off, too. Having her other son disappear at this point would have been more than she could handle.

Rachel kept her eyes glued to the door as her heart pounded frantically.

A middle-aged policeman stepped inside. "Still no sign of them, Mrs. Murdock," he said, glancing at her and shaking his head regretfully. "But we're not giving up yet. In fact, we've expanded our search. Kids can sometimes wander off to the darndest places. I'm sure we'll be finding them soon."

A burning sensation at the pit of Rachel's stomach intensified, but, in spite of the ache, she managed to nod in the officer's direction. Jorgie slipped from the chair he had been sitting on at the dining table and, without looking at anyone in particular, said in a low, uncertain voice that he was going outside on the patio for a while.

Rachel's whole body tensed at the thought of her son going anywhere at all out of her sight—even for a moment. But then she took a deep, calming breath and told herself that nothing was going to happen to him. For heaven's sake, he was just walking out onto her patio.

Besides, she knew that now wasn't the time to let herself forget her real motive for moving to Louisi-

ana with her children. In truth, she had done so with
the hope that they would learn to lead normal, ordinary lives again, far away from the atmosphere where
money and power were considered the ultimate prize
in life and the price of success was never too great.
Indeed, if money could've bought them happiness and
the world actually did turn on a gold coin like Ross
and so many of his friends thought, then the Murdock family would have been bursting at the seams in
joy. Instead they were simply busted up. For Rachel,
that in itself was all the proof she needed to arm herself and to protect her sons from a way of life that had
already brought her so much unhappiness.

And yet, even here, in the quiet of her small, laid-
back hometown of Abbeville, Louisiana, it seemed
she'd failed in protecting her children.

Swallowing hard, she gave her older son a fleeting
smile. "Just don't leave the backyard, Jorgie. Not for
any reason, okay?"

He nodded.

After Jorgie walked out the back door, Rachel
glanced at the policeman and saw that one corner of
his mouth was lifted in a simple smile that said he understood her concern for Jorgie's safety. "Mrs. Murdock, there's another officer out here on the patio and
he's going to remain for the time being. I'll tell him to
keep an eye on your son. So try to relax, okay?"

"Thank you," Rachel replied, returning a weak
smile of her own. But right now relaxing was impossible for her, and it was useless to even try. Instead she
clasped her hands even tighter in her lap and sighed
heavily.

Once again her thoughts turned to Ross. Actually,
even now, when their lives were so separate and she

was planning to divorce him, he was seldom very far from her mind. Over the years he had become such an interwoven part of her, that it wasn't an easy task to suddenly get him unraveled just because it was what she needed to do. In fact, so far, it seemed, she'd made very little progress, regardless of her efforts.

Suddenly realizing that she was on the verge of recalling some rather painful memories, Rachel quickly focused her thoughts on the present. After all, this moment wasn't about her. It was about her son, and she yearned to hold him in her arms and know that he was safe.

Taking a deep breath, Rachel glanced at her wristwatch and frowned. Then, suddenly she heard the distinct voices of several adults talking outside on her patio. "I'm not giving up until my son and his friend are found," she heard one of the voices say, and knew instantly and instinctively that the voice belonged to Ross. As a result, something pulled hard and deep inside of her. "Have another search party ready in five minutes," he added a moment later. By now, Rachel's heart was pounding wildly.

She knew that Ross would be coming inside and decided to rise from her seated position at the kitchen table. But before she could, the back door swung wide open and the tall, lean-muscled man she was expecting to see stepped in. Mesmerized, Rachel watched as he stopped just inside the doorway and brought his hands to his hips. His presence seemed to overwhelm everything around him.

And then, as she sat there in a daze, the same old familiar feeling that always left her breathless when he entered the room regenerated itself and began to swirl through the air like an invisible gas. That sensation, along with the fact that maybe…just maybe now that Ross had finally arrived, he would be the one to find their missing son and his friend, left Rachel feeling almost light-headed.

The room grew deafeningly silent.

His dark brown eyes settled on her face.

Rachel felt her insides quaver.

And in that moment she realized something she hated having to admit to herself. That even at a time like this, Ross still had the same sexual appeal for her that he always had. In truth, she was still hopelessly in love with a man who no longer needed her in his life. It was that simple. And that sad. But it was also a reality that she had no choice but to accept.

His eyes narrowed as they focused on her.

Rachel opened her mouth to speak, but she didn't know quite what to say at this point. When she'd walked out on her marriage six months ago, she'd deliberately drawn lines to separate Ross's world from hers and then promised herself that she wasn't going to cross over to his side ever again. But she hadn't anticipated this moment, when her need for comfort of any kind would be so strong.

Still, even at such a critical time as this, the last thing she wanted was to appear weak in his eyes. Because she wasn't weak. Her mother had been weak. Her mother had allowed her father to treat her like dirt and then had fallen completely apart when he'd finally left her. Rachel Murdock was not going to let any man get away with that. Not even the man she adored.

Snapping back to the present, Rachel quickly decided her best avenue was to sit still and wait to see what Ross's next move would be.

Within a fraction of that moment, Ross took a step forward and the door shut on its own behind him, blocking out the bright light from the patio that had beamed in through its opening, framing him in light and somehow making him appear like a god standing there before her, less than fifteen feet away. Only now she could see the lines of worry etched on his face and the look was all too human.

The truth of the matter was, with all of the millions he'd earned over the past ten years, with all the prestige and power that now clung to him like medals of valor pinned to his breast pocket, the only thing she had ever truly wanted from him was his everlasting love and commitment to her and their children. That's it. Period. But somewhere along the way to gaining personal and financial success, Ross Murdock had stripped the word *everlasting* from his vocabulary.

Suddenly, hot, brutal tears sprang to Rachel's eyes and she bit down on her bottom lip in an effort to stall them.

Ross began to move in her direction and a moment later the distance between them was quickly eaten up. Reaching her, and in a voice filled with emotion, he said, "Dammit, Rachel, this is crazy. If you don't need to be held, that's fine. But I need to hold you."

And then she was in his strong arms, being held against his hard body, which easily supported her additional weight without wavering. Her body trembled against his and she clung to him with every ounce of strength she possessed. With one side of her face pressed against his chest, she could hear the hard, consistent *thumping* of his heart. Then, after savoring the bittersweet moment for as long as she could without having him think that she was a clinging vine, she finally pulled back and looked up at him. "Oh, Ross, I can't believe this is happening. I'm so sorry."

Ross immediately released his hold around her waist and gathered her face in his hands. "Hey, come on now, Rachel, pull yourself together. This isn't your fault. It's mine," he replied.

Rachel's eyes widened. "It's not your fault," she exclaimed in an emotional tone of voice.

"Well, it damned sure isn't yours."

"I wish I could believe that, but I can't," Rachel said, attempting to shake her head from side to side, but his hands held her firmly in place. "I should've been watching him more closely. But—"

Rachel paused for a deep, steadying breath. "But it was like one minute he and Orlan were here in the backyard playing, and then in the next, they were gone. I thought they had walked over to Orlan's house. And Mindy, Orlan's mother, thought they were still here." Rachel's features tightened as she fought back additional tears. "When I saw that they were gone, I went to check with her right away, but it was already too late. We looked all over the place, but we couldn't find them anywhere." Finally her face crumpled. "That was over eight hours ago. Oh, Ross, I'm so frightened for them."

His arms went around her once more and he held her close. "Hey, come on now, Rachel. You've got to listen to me. They're going to be all right. I'm here now and I'm not going to give up until I find them."

Rachel's eyes widened. Ross sounded so sure of himself—and she desperately wanted to believe his every word. But common sense told her that he was only doing the same as everyone else. In reality, he couldn't offer her any more of a guarantee of Danny's safe return than the police could. However, once upon a time she had believed so completely in him that she had thought him capable of doing anything. And, somewhere deep down inside, she still did.

Rachel's heart was pounding wildly. "But the police have been searching everywhere."

"I know. But a kid like Danny can go off to just about anywhere."

Rachel shook her head. "But Danny would've come home by now. And what about Orlan? I'm telling you, Ross, something has happened to them."

"Try not to jump to all kinds of conclusions, Rachel. You'll only end up making things worse on yourself. We're going to find them safe."

Rachel inhaled deeply and then held it. "Do you really think so?" she asked hopefully.

Ross gave her a halfhearted smile. "You know what I really think?" he said, suddenly rubbing the backside of his fingers down her cheek and throwing what few rational thoughts she had left in her head completely out of whack.

"No. What?" Rachel asked. In that moment she was just desperate enough to want to believe in anything he might have to say. She had once needed this man so much. Obviously, in some ways she still did, and probably always would. It was just such a pity that he didn't feel the same about her any longer.

The corners of Ross's mouth lifted in a slight smile. "Look, I bet anything that Danny and his friend slipped off together on purpose. And when their energy finally gave out, they sat down for a while under some big old shade tree and fell asleep. I bet you that someone is going to stumble upon them at any moment." He shook her gently by the shoulders. "Now you've got to believe that, Rachel. For Danny's sake, and for ours.''

The same police officer from earlier knocked on the back door and then came inside. "I'm ready when you are, Mr. Murdock. I have the map now. I can show you exactly where we've already searched."

Ross glanced back over his shoulder at the man. "I'll be out in a second." The officer nodded and went back outside. Turning his attention to Rachel once again, Ross squeezed her shoulders. "I'll find Danny. I promise." Then he kissed her lightly on the forehead and walked out.

The kiss had been brief, and Rachel knew it was something he'd done from habit. No way did she believe that he was feeling as raw and as needy inside as she was. Ross Murdock had never needed anyone that badly in his life.

Stressed now to the point of nausea, Rachel followed Ross to the door and watched as he joined the search party that consisted mostly of her neighbors and volunteer off-duty policemen and firemen. They all gathered around the officer in charge and listened intently to the instructions being given.

With her gaze focused on Ross, Rachel folded her arms across her middle and leaned against the door frame. Tears gathered in her eyes as she watched him head out with the others. Eventually, though, she lost sight of him and knew that it was pointless for her to continue standing there, staring into the dark night. But before returning to the kitchen table to keep her vigil, she paused for a moment longer and began to pray....

Please, God, she whispered in the solitude of her heart, whatever it was that she or Ross, or both of them had done wrong to break apart their marriage, punish them for it, not their innocent little boy.

And if, in some way, by some miracle or chance, she could have been assured of Ross's love for all time, she was undoubtedly weak enough in that moment that she would have asked for that, too.

Chapter Two

Two long, agonizing hours passed, and now midnight was approaching with no word from Ross or any of the others who were still out searching for Danny and Orlan. However, the fact that Ross was one of the people still out there somewhere, looking for their son, gave Rachel the single shred of hope she held on to. To Ross's credit, she knew that he had more determination in his one little finger than most people had in their entire body. He'd said that he wasn't going to come back without Danny and Orlan, and, for her own peace of mind, Rachel had to believe that was true.

Jorgie was asleep on the sofa, while Jan and two of her neighbors from down the block were keeping vigil by sitting together at the kitchen table and sipping black coffee. Rachel had already drunk so much of the stuff, the thought of forcing down another swallow was nauseating. In fact, after feeling the need to be alone for a few moments, she'd slipped out the front door of her house without bothering to tell anyone where she was going and was now sitting on the edge of her porch, with her legs crisscrossed under her and her hands folded in her lap.

All day long Jan had kept telling her that she was in a state of shock, and Rachel supposed her sister was correct. In one split second her whole world had turned upside down, and no matter how hard she tried, she couldn't get it right side up, again. Right now, only one thing could accomplish that.

A renewed batch of hot tears pooled in Rachel's eyes. Telling herself, however, that she needed to remain strong, regardless of her exhaustion, she finally sucked in a deep breath, wiped away the moisture on her face and found the necessary courage to renew her flagging hopes. It was still possible for Danny and Orlan to be found unharmed. The police said the first twenty-four hours were the most critical in any search to find a missing person. There was still plenty of time, and still plenty of margin for hope. She had to believe that.

And so, as the quiet calm of midnight took a firm grip on the area, Rachel sat there in silence and listened to the melancholic, echoing sounds of the ever-constant choir of insects that claimed south Louisiana as their native home. From the sanctuary of a nearby flower bed, a misplaced bullfrog mistook her small cemented birdbath for a pond and belched out its mating call in the hopes that a female would come to him. Normally, Rachel loved this time of night. Normally, it had a peaceful, calming effect on her. But on this particular evening, the mating call of insects and animals alike only made her feel all the more

lonely inside. All she could think of was how Danny
had missed his supper and was probably getting hungry by now. And, not only that, but it looked as
though he might end up missing a safe, good night's
sleep in his own bed, too...

Oh, God, she could hardly stand this waiting...and waiting. It was driving her crazy.

Suddenly, as though the hand of fate had just in-
tervened in her thoughts, Rachel turned her head and
saw that someone was fast approaching her through
the darkness. A moment later she recognized him as
her older neighbor from across the street. The last time
she had seen him, he was leaving with the same search
party that had included Ross.

Her heart was the first to react to the sight of him,
slamming itself against her breastbone. Meanwhile,
the remainder of her body stayed frozen to the spot.

Smiling as he reached her, the neighbor pointed
down the block in the direction he had just come.
"Look down yonder, Mrs. Murdock, and you're sure
enough gonna see a sight for sore eyes. Yessirree, a
real sight for sore eyes."

Stunned by the suddenness of it all, and therefore
slow at first to react to his statement, Rachel could
only frown in confusion. Finally his words sank in and
she sprang from the edge of the porch and dashed
down the sidewalk toward the curb. She heard him
chuckling as he followed close behind, and the fact
that he had been able to laugh during a critical moment such as this somehow lightened the emotional
overload she was carrying with her.

By this time, with the aid of the bright overhead
streetlights, Rachel instantly recognized the approaching group and her heart fell to her knees. It was

a few seconds more, however, before she was finally able to recognize Ross as the one in the lead.

Well, actually, it wasn't his facial features so much that she was able to recognize through the dimness of night. It was Ross's gait that she knew as well as her own. Then, suddenly, as she continued to observe him, she realized that he was carrying a child.

"Danny?" she said out loud as big tears reassembled in her eyes, blurring her vision. Gut instinct drove her to start walking at a fast pace in their direction. But after a brief moment even that wasn't fast enough and she broke into a jog.

Ross saw Rachel's silhouette at a distance, coming toward them through the shadows cast by the overhead streetlights. He knew it was her. She was his wife, for heaven's sake. He'd made love to her too many times in the past for him not to know her body as well as his own. At any distance. At any time of day or night. In truth, there wasn't a secret part of her that his fingers hadn't explored, or his lips hadn't tasted. He knew his way around her every flaw and her every perfection. And even now when he was both physically and emotionally drained, he wanted her as much as he ever had—as much as any man could possibly ever want a woman.

These last few hours had given him a whole lot of time to do some really hard thinking about his life, about the mistakes he'd made and about what he needed to do to make up for them. It wasn't easy for a man like himself to turn loose of his hefty pride and admit to the world that he'd screwed up royally, but he had. No wonder Rachel had taken their children and run away from him. He'd become so wrapped up in his gold-foiled world that he'd taken everything in his life for granted. He couldn't even count how many family birthdays and anniversary celebrations he'd forgotten over the years. He'd been a real self-centered bastard, all right.

But all of that was going to change now. Today's crisis—along with the past six months of some rather thorough soul-searching—had finally pried open his eyes to the kind of man he'd really become. And now he wanted his wife back. And his kids. And his old way of life. The one that he and Rachel had had in the beginning of their marriage. The one he'd almost single-handedly destroyed. He was just thankful that he'd awakened in time. And now the real challenge was going to be convincing Rachel of that fact.

Lord knew, it wasn't going to be easy. Because if there was one thing he could say about his wife, it was that she wasn't—nor, had she ever been—easy. She'd always been complicated and passionate—and downright stubborn at times. In truth, she was the one woman in all the world who could bring him to his knees.

Still and all, he'd been a real jerk, and winning her back was going to be his biggest challenge ever. Therefore he'd used his time while searching for Danny to devise himself a plan of action. Starting now, at this very moment, he was going to shower Rachel with all the affection she deserved, and by doing so he hoped to open her eyes to the fact that he was now a changed man. A man who had learned a cold, hard lesson in life that he would never forget.

"Look, Danny," he said to his son a moment later, pointing in Rachel's direction, "there's your mommy. Didn't I tell you that she was coming?"

By now, Rachel was upon them, crying as she gathered Danny into her arms and hugged him tight. It was an emotional moment, flanked by all the previous hours of excess worry and exhaustion on everyone's part, and as the rescuers gathered around the reunion of mother and son, their eyes grew damp. Orlan's mother arrived during the middle of that scene and her reunion with her son was equally absorbing.

For the benefit of the two mothers who had just arrived, the police officer in charge gave a brief account of the boys' rescue.

Danny and Orlan hadn't been lost or kidnapped, as everyone had once feared. Instead they'd gotten themselves trapped in the loft of an old abandoned barn less than two miles up the road. Somehow the ladder they'd used to climb up had gotten knocked to the ground. Orlan, it seemed, had already been warned by the owner of the property that he was going to be arrested if he was caught inside the dilapidated old building again. So, naturally, when Orlan saw the police searching the area, he relayed that information to Danny and they became frightened of being arrested and taken to jail. Of course, the owner hadn't meant what he'd said. He'd only meant to scare Orlan away, but his tactic had ended up backfiring on the child. And whenever the police or other volunteers had come near the barn in search of them, Orlan and Danny had hidden from view and not made a sound until Danny had heard his father calling to him. Realizing he was safe, he'd answered back, and within minutes Ross had them down from the hayloft.

The story of her son's adventure was an incredible tale. But regardless of where he had been during those dreadful, frantic hours, Rachel felt truly blessed to now have him back with her.

She owed Ross a debt of gratitude. The police had made it perfectly clear that if Ross hadn't been there as a part of the rescue efforts, Danny and Orlan might not have been found as quickly. Even if Ross had been delayed an hour after receiving her phone call, it was very possible that Danny and Orlan could have ended up spending the entire night in that old smelly loft.

With their mission accomplished, one by one, the tired and hungry rescuers began to depart for home. When the final volunteer walked away, Ross followed the one remaining police officer to his car and they spoke quietly for several minutes. In the meantime, Rachel decided to plop down on the ground under a streetlight, next to the curb. Danny immediately sat in her lap and by the time she looked up to see Ross walking toward them, Danny's tired little body had already begun to relax against her and Rachel knew that he had fallen sound asleep.

Ross approached, and Rachel glanced up at him. "My legs gave out," she said in a tired voice, "so I decided to have a seat."

He grinned. "Careful, kitten. There's a hungry tiger out here. He just might end up nipping off the end of your cute little nose."

She sobered instantly. Rachel wasn't certain what he'd meant by that, but then again, she wasn't going to ask him, either. She glanced down at the child in her lap. "Danny's fallen a-asleep," she stammered.

Bending at the knees, Ross dropped down to their level. "I can see that," he replied, running his fingers through his son's hair, pulling out some straw. He wiped a smudge of dirt from Danny's cheek and then wrinkled up his own nose. "Pooh-wee," he said laughingly. "He needs a bath. He smells like an old barnyard dog."

In spite of herself, Rachel smiled at that remark. "I noticed. But I don't care. It feels too wonderful to hold him again and know that he's safe."

Ross smiled. "I have to agree with that. Still, he's gonna smell a whole lot better when we get him home and cleaned up."

"He could care less," Rachel commented with a hint of a smile still on her lips.

Ross gazed down at Danny for the longest time. Finally he said, "You know, I think he's beginning to look more and more like you."

That remark forced a quick laugh from Rachel. "Oh, no, Ross. You're wrong about that. Danny's the spitting image of you." She ran a gentle finger over her son's features. "Look at the shape of his nose, the way his chin squares off. And see his hairline? It's straight across, just like yours," Rachel said. She looked up at Ross and their eyes met. And suddenly she felt breathless for no apparent reason. "Actually, everything about him reminds me of you. Even the way he walks—a-and talks."

"Oh, yeah?" Ross said, leaning in proudly and finally dropping his eyes away from hers to get a better look at his son. He examined Danny more closely. "Well, maybe you're right," he replied at last. "Still, there's something about him that reminds me of you."

Once again his eyes lifted to Rachel's, and as a result, she found that her chest squeezed tight. "Well, I should hope so," she replied, trying desperately to make light of a moment that was growing increasingly too heavy for her liking. "He's a part of me, too, you know."

Ross gave her a playful, sexy little grin that slipped up one side of his face. "So it *was* you that night."

Rachel gaped and then swatted him on the arm when she realized that he was teasing her. Ross had hurt her in a lot of ways over the years. But, as far as she knew, he'd never been unfaithful to her. Not yet, anyway. But she had seen all the signs and believed eventually he would've, just as her father had. And that would have destroyed her, just as her father's betrayal had destroyed her mother so long ago.

"Well, maybe our next baby will look like you," Ross said, drawing her attention back to the moment. Blinking twice, she saw that he was smiling at her. "Maybe it'll be a little girl."

Rachel's breath caught in her throat. In her heart she felt certain the child she had miscarried last year had been a little girl. And she had wanted her so much. So much, in fact, that sometimes her arms still ached to hold her.

Still, she couldn't allow herself to get caught up in those painful memories right now. Already it had been a year since that fretful night when she'd begun to hemorrhage and had had to go to the emergency room alone, without her husband, because he had been away on another one of his infamous business trips. Already a year since she had lost what would have been her third child, as well as any faith she might have still had that their marriage would somehow stand the test of time. In essence, it had been the final straw for her.

Rachel jerked herself back into the present as a chill shivered down her spine.

Ross's gaze intensified. "What's wrong?"

Rachel glanced down at Danny. "Nothing."

He placed his fingers under her chin and tilted it upward. "Are you sure?"

"Positive."

Ross studied her for a long moment in a way that told her that he knew what she had been thinking about. "Rachel, I'm so sorry about the baby. I—I..."

Rachel's heart felt as though it was breaking into pieces all over again, and a part of her wanted to throw herself into her husband's strong arms and tell him to never let her go. But the other part of her, the one that was angry and confused, refused to allow her to be so weak. It told her to tighten her resolve and hold her head up high. "I think we'd better get Danny home," she heard herself saying in a cool voice.

Ross gazed at her for the longest time before sighing heavily. "Look, Rachel, I know I let you down in the past. But it doesn't matter what you say, or how far you try to run from me today, every time you turn around, I'm going to be there, right behind you and the kids."

A dark shadow fell across Rachel's features. "You have no idea how many times my father gave my mother a line similar to that one."

"Maybe she should've believed him."

"Oh, but she did. Every time he said it. Let's see, just how many times did she swallow her pride and take him back?"

"But I'm not your father, Rachel."

Throwing up her guards like shields between herself and the enemy, Rachel glared at him. "Well, I'm not my mother, that's for sure. So don't expect me to believe every single word you say."

Disappointed in her reaction, he glared back. "Well, you're wrong about me. And I'm going to prove it."

Rachel shrugged. "It's a free country. You can do as you please. But I don't have to like it." Then, keeping her emotional guards in place, Rachel gave him a complacent look. "I think it's time we get Danny home now, don't you?"

After giving her a lingering gaze, Ross scooted in closer. "Hand him over to me and I'll carry him."

"All right," Rachel replied, her expression passive. She immediately shifted Danny to a position that she thought would make it easy for Ross to lift him from her lap.

"Come here, sport," Ross said, leaning forward.

In Rachel's attempt to help Ross, she held on to Danny for as long as she could—which ended up being for too long. As a result Ross's upper arm rubbed back and forth over her breasts a couple of times, and her nipples reacted by squeezing tight.

Ross's gaze shot to her face. "Sorry," he said.

Rachel blushed. "It's okay."

"I didn't hurt you, did I?"

Suddenly that same old awareness in her, the one that had made her pick him above all others, jumped in its red, convertible hot rod and took a wild, sensuous cruise down her main artery, leaving her with an exhilarating high that almost shattered her composure. Her face blushed. "No," she said with a shortness of breath that she tried desperately to hide from him. But his grin said that she hadn't fooled him one little bit.

"You sure?" he asked. "I thought I heard you groan."

Rachel shook her head. "That wasn't a groan."

Ross frowned. "Sure sounded like a groan to me," he replied, giving her an intense, level look. "But I guess I could be wrong. Who knows, maybe it was actually a moan. Let me see if I can still get this straight about you... You groan when you're hurt and you moan when you're turned on." His face suddenly brightened. "Hey, are you turned on, by any chance?"

Deepening her blush, Rachel looked off to one side.

"Well, I'll be damned," Ross said, pretending to suffer from a moment of stunned disbelief. But Rachel wasn't buying it for a second and refused to even glance in his direction. He was probably gloating, anyway. But then, regardless of her intentions, a moment later he placed his fingers under her chin and turned her face to examine it. A slow grin eased across his mouth—just like she had known it would. "Why, Rachel Murdock, I do believe you're blushing."

"All right," Rachel said, immediately pulling herself free of his hold. "The fun on my account is now officially over. This conversation has already gone past the limit of protocol. Therefore, you can stay here all night long if you like, but I'm going home now." Having said that, Rachel attempted to stand, but Ross quickly clamped his wide hand on her shoulder and shoved her buttocks back down to the ground.

"Not so fast, kitten," he said, a grin turning up the corners of what Rachel had always thought was a very sensuous-looking mouth. Too sensuous for her own good, in fact. But his lips were the absolute last thing she needed to be thinking about right now.

"Ouch, Ross," she snapped, rubbing her backside with the palm of her hand. "That hurt."

"I'm sorry. You need more padding, kitten."

"Sure I do, but only if I decide to become a female wrestler."

"I said I was sorry."

"Yeah, right," Rachel said, eyeing his amused features. His dark brown eyes twinkled with mischief. "And you really look it, too."

His grin widened. "Listen, my legs are starting to give out, so I'm not going to be able to stay squatted down in this position much longer."

"Then, get up. Who's stopping you?"

His eyes darkened. "I have a question I want to ask you first."

"The answer's no."

He laughed, showing white, even teeth. "You don't even know the question yet."

Rachel wished that he didn't have so much sex appeal. It would have made her life so much easier. "And I don't want to know it."

"Sorry, kid," he said, though actually looking anything but remorseful. "But I can't let you get off the hook that easily." Then his expression changed to one of sincerity. "Look, we've both been through the wringer, today. Therefore, I'd like very much to take you out tomorrow night for a nice, quiet dinner for two. Champagne, dancing to some slow, sexy music—the works. You name it, we'll experience it. It'll be a night on the town to remember. What do you say, Rachel? Let's do it."

Rachel gazed at him sideways. "And just what else do you have in mind for us to do?"

He shrugged, all innocentlike. "I haven't the slightest idea what you mean by that."

Rachel gave a sight smirk. "Oh, I think you do."

A sexy little grin slipped across his face.

Rachel narrowed her eyes.

"Well . . ." he finally drawled, "as a matter of fact, maybe I was hoping that it wouldn't end just there. You know me, I always did enjoy your nightcaps."

In spite of herself, Rachel found herself amused at his honesty. Of course, he'd had no choice in the matter. He knew she knew him too well to have believed otherwise of him. "Well, I can assure you that there wouldn't be any nightcap this time, Ross. We're separated, remember?"

"Actually, kitten, you make it pretty darn impossible for me to forget."

"Good," she replied. "'Cause I'm trying to see to it that you don't."

Giving her a hard, level stare, Ross finally sighed. Then, tightening his hold on Danny, he eased away from Rachel and attempted to rise. But suddenly he lost his footing and toppled forward into Rachel, knocking her down, flat against the ground. He and Danny landed on top of her.

Rachel groaned. Ross grunted. But, Danny, who was now sandwiched between them, didn't even waken from his sound sleep. Not even when Ross regained his balance, pulled himself onto his knees and lifted Danny into his arms once again. Rachel watched as Ross placed their son on the ground right next to her. In fact, she was still looking at Danny when Ross suddenly said, "Well, now, it seems I've finally gotten you where I've been wanting you all along."

Rachel swung her wide eyes to his smiling face and instantly discovered that he had somehow managed to maneuver himself so that he now straddled her. Holding her hands against the ground on either side of her head, and using his muscular thighs to hold her hips firmly in place, he continued to give her that mischievous grin of his. In truth, a grin she hadn't seen on his face in a long, long time. "You're at my mercy, now, Rachel Murdock. I give you three seconds to plead your case."

Her eyes grew round. "You're crazy."

"One . . ." he counted. "Two . . ."

"But . . . but . . . wait . . ."

"Three. Ah, sorry, kiddo. But your three seconds are already up." ·

"Ross, this is ridiculous. Have you lost your mind?"

"Possibly."

"Will you please get off me before the neighbors see us like this and wonder what in the world we're doing out here on the ground?"

"So let 'em wonder. What's the big deal? We've both had a tough day. We deserve a little fun."

"Balloons and ice cream and pin the donkey's tail are fun."

"Well, hey, I'm no party pooper. We can have that, too, once we get Danny home."

"Ross, be serious. I live in this neighborhood. I know that people are watching us at this very moment."

"I am being serious. You're the one who isn't taking my offer seriously. I asked you nicely to have dinner with me and you haven't even bothered to give me an answer."

"Okay, then. The answer's no."

His expression sobered instantly. "Why not?"

"Because we're separated, for heaven's sake."

His frown deepened. "So?"

"So, dining and dancing—and anything else that you have in mind for us to do together—well, it simply isn't the proper protocol for separated couples."

"Says who?"

"Says... whomever," Rachel replied when suddenly she couldn't think straight to come up with a name.

"Do you know what I think about your so-called protocol?"

"No, and I'd really rather not know."

His frown vanished and a playful expression replaced it. "Well, I think it stinks. Besides, some rules are made to be broken."

"Not this one," Rachel replied, keeping a tight rein on her emotions. In truth, she longed for any kind of a night on the town with him. Actually, a part of her still longed for a lifetime with him, and probably always would.

Just then a car passed them and the driver honked the horn several times as the vehicle continued traveling down the block at a slow rate of speed. Rolling the window down, a teenager on the passenger side stuck his head out, shouted an obscenity and then gave an ear-piercing whistle that woke up the entire dog population in the neighborhood and got them to barking.

Rachel glared at Ross accusingly. "Now see what you've done," she said in a hurried, aggravated tone of voice. "With all that horn-blowing and whistling and barking going on out here, my neighbors are sure to see us."

Ross grinned. "Sounds to me like we've gone to the dogs."

"My thoughts exactly. Now get off of me so I can move."

"No way. Not without a kiss first."

"You're nuts."

"And you're cute."

Rachel rolled her eyes and Ross laughed at her. "Look," he said, "maybe I ought to enlighten you as to how this situation is actually summing up.

"You see," he continued a moment later, giving her just a hint of a smile, "Danny's sound asleep, so he could care less where he is right now. And it just so happens that I've got all night. So, if you want to drag this out, Danny and I both have all the time in the world. Therefore, you just might find yourself right here, flat on your back, all night long. So, what's it gonna be, kitten? One small kiss from you—or an all-night standoff?"

Boy, some choice he was giving her, Rachel thought. In fact, it was no choice at all.

Eventually, just as she had figured, Ross's diehard determination won out over hers and Rachel resigned herself to the fact that she'd lost this one battle. But graciously? Uh-uh. No way. She still had her pride, and just enough of a fiery temper to annoy him. Therefore, closing her eyes tightly, she puckered her lips and then waited for what she thought was the inevitable.

And she waited.

And then waited some more.

But nothing happened.

Finally she began to wonder if she'd somehow missed the kiss altogether and decided to take a peek at her surroundings. Opening one eye, she saw that Ross's face was only a couple of inches from hers. "Well, what are you waiting for?" she asked. "Aren't you going to kiss me?"

Ross laughed huskily. "Oh, sure, kitten. I plan to kiss you, all right. I just wanted to give you time to think about it first."

"What's there to think about?" She puckered up once more. "Go ahead. Get it over with," she said, squeezing her lips together.

"Just remember," he said meaningfully, "you asked for it."

Rachel's eyes flew open. "I most certainly did not," she replied. "This is all your doing, not mine."

His mouth was now less than an inch from hers.

"Rachel."

"What?"

"Will you please just shut up and kiss me?"

Rachel had no earthly idea why she was so willing to now cooperate with him. Something was driving her, she supposed. Something—perhaps a certain look in his eyes—that made her feel this growing need to be kissed. And so, with pulses accelerating to an all-time high, Rachel closed her eyes one more time and waited. Finally, just as she had reached the point of taking another peek, she felt his warm lips cover hers.

In the beginning the kiss was tender and sweet. But then all too soon his tongue became enticingly wicked and teased and tasted every single inch of her inner mouth with the intimate knowledge of a former lover. In truth, her only lover.

Her blood thickened. Curdled. Boiled. And then thinned again, so that it now flowed through her veins like a raging river.

Ross held her hands firmly above her head and ground the hard, lower part of his body against hers in a slow, enticing motion. Rachel's belly burned with need and, when finally he released her, she wrapped her arms around his waist and held him against her all the more.

Ross's moves were smooth and efficient. Within moments he had stroked and manipulated her growing passion with expert precision. Soon his mouth slipped away from hers and sought the fullness of one ample breast. And when his mouth closed over her—clothing and all—she moaned in sweet agony.

And then, suddenly, as though she had just seen the signs of enlightenment in the sky above, Rachel remembered where she was and who she was with—and what, in heaven's name, they were doing—and she sobered as quickly as a Sunday morning preacher making a television debut. Placing the palms of her hands at Ross's shoulders, she said, "Ross, stop..." And then she gave him a hard shove.

Rachel's sudden move startled Ross, and he pulled back to look at her. A moment later he was on his feet, offering her his hand to get up. Ignoring it, she rose on her own accord and began dusting off the particles of grass and dust that clung to the back of her clothes.

"Look, I'm sorry, Rachel," Ross said. "I know I went too far. I didn't mean for the kiss to get so out of hand."

"Like hell you didn't," she replied without looking up at him.

"Look, it's true. It just sort of exploded out of control."

"Yeah, sure," she replied. Still, she kept her eyes focused elsewhere.

Dropping his hands to his sides, Ross clenched his jaw. "Come on," he said. "It's time to get Danny home." At that point he picked up Danny, turned and began heading towards her house. Danny's arm tightened around his neck and it was then Ross realized that his son wasn't as sound asleep as he and Rachel had thought.

Rachel fell into step alongside him in silence. Soon they arrived at her doorstep, and Jorgie and Jan came running out to greet them. Rachel assured everyone that Danny was all right and, while Ross entered the front door with his son still asleep on his shoulder, she explained the circumstances of the rescue. After that, Rachel's two neighbors who had been sitting in the kitchen with Jan went on home.

"So both Danny and Orlan are all right?" Jan asked.

"Yes, thank heaven," Rachel replied.

Ross turned to face Rachel. "Where do you want me to put Danny?"

Following Rachel's instructions, Ross carried Danny to the hall bathroom where Rachel joined him a few moments later. Within minutes they had their youngest son bathed and dressed in a clean pair of pajamas. Danny woke up for the bath but once he was warm and dry and had taken a few sips of milk, opted for bed right away. Jorgie was tucked in, too. Ushering Rachel and Ross out of the boys' bedroom to take care of their own needs, Jan offered to linger behind with the boys until they were asleep.

In truth, Rachel was more exhausted than she was hungry, and couldn't wait to take a shower and go to bed. But, knowing Ross as she did, she knew that he was probably famished and felt it was her duty to see to it that he got something to eat before he left her house to find a place to spend the rest of the night. It was the least she could do, after all.

Going into the kitchen, she busied herself with the task of fixing them each a plate of leftovers and then heated them up in the microwave oven. At some moment she became increasingly aware that she was being observed rather thoroughly. She turned to discover Ross leaning against the nearby counter, his arms folded across his chest, gazing at her with such an intensity that a sudden heat began to rise from her lower abdomen. It was the kind of heat that dried her mouth and forced her eyes to unwillingly follow his every move.

Whirling around, she turned back to her task and then got busy washing a couple of dirty glasses. Finally, after clearing her throat of a kind of breathlessness, she glanced back at him. "Ross, there are some canned drinks in the fridge. Would you mind getting us each one?"

"Sure thing," he replied, lazily strolling to the white, double-door refrigerator with its door-front water dispenser. He pulled open one of the doors and peered inside.

"Check the bottom shelf," she said, setting their plates of food down on the table. She turned back to shut the microwave door and found that her heart was pounding like crazy. Like she was just now experiencing a profound attraction to him for the first time ever. Which was absurd in itself. Her attraction to him had started years ago, when they were both still in high school.

When she realized that Ross's movements had grown awfully quiet and he hadn't answered her yet, she glanced back and saw that he held something in his hand...a glass bottle, she thought, that was light brown or amber in color. Whatever it was, he was carefully scrutinizing the label. Having absolutely no idea what he'd discovered in her refrigerator—she certainly didn't recognize the glass container as something she'd purchased at the grocer—she frowned curiously. "Ross, what is that?"

It took him a second before he finally bothered to glance up at her, but when he did, their gazes collided like two rockets fired from opposing forces. In fact, the intensity in his hit her like a shotgun blast and she stilled as though she'd been shot.

"That's strange," he drawled, instantly developing a definite, sarcastic attitude that she found profoundly irritating. "But I was about to ask you the same thing."

Puzzled now even more—*what was his problem, anyway?*—Rachel dropped the damp dish cloth she'd used to wipe up some crumbs near the sink and walked over to where he stood. With a certain, almost irritating preciseness, Ross positioned the amber-colored bottle so that she could read the label. After getting only a glimpse of it, she looked up and shrugged. "I don't get it, Ross. It's only a bottle of beer. So what's the big deal?"

"Only a bottle of beer," Ross repeated sarcastically. "See, that's what I don't get. It's only a bottle of beer."

Dumbfounded, Rachel deepened her frown. "So?"

"So, you don't drink beer," he replied in a chastising tone of voice. "Or, at least, you didn't used to."

"Well...I—I do sometimes," she finally stammered.

"But not very often. And not this brand. I know that for a fact. I remember we tried it once and you hated the taste."

Rachel shrugged. "Well, why disagree with you? You seem to know more about my taste in beer than I do."

Ross didn't appear intimidated by her comment at all. Nor did he seem in the least bit remorseful for being such a jerk over a bottle of beer, for heaven's sake. "Where did it come from, Rachel?"

Again, she shrugged. "How would I know?"

"How? Because it was in your refrigerator, that's how."

"Well, I don't remember buying it for myself, that's for sure."

"Oh...? Well, if you don't remember buying it for yourself, then who do you remember buying it for?"

Rachel felt that same old awareness of him begin to escalate. Only this time it left her breathless and in need of something from him she would have preferred not to have recognized. Not if she still planned to go through with divorcing him. Which, of course, she did. "What is this, Ross, the third degree?"

"No," he said, practically snapping off her head with his arrogant tone of voice. "No third degree. Just be straightforward with me and answer the question."

"Okay, then, dammit," she replied, placing her hands on her hips. "I will."

Giving her a smug, satisfied look, Ross set the bottle on the counter and, mimicking her, placed his hands on his hips. "Well..." he said impatiently. "I'm waiting for your answer."

Chapter Three

Rachel gaped at Ross. In all honesty, she couldn't believe his audacity. When he'd had a right to question her about who her friends were, he could have cared less. And now, well...she simply didn't feel she owed him that much. Not anymore.

"Ross, let me make myself perfectly clear this time. I don't recall buying any beer for me or for anyone, okay?" Suddenly, a spark of true-blue irritation flickered to life in her. And why not? This conversation was so utterly ridiculous, it was frustrating. She was tired of being on the defensive. Especially when the reason was so senseless. "And to be perfectly frank with you, I don't think it's any of your damned business."

Ross's face lost all expression and he stared at her blankly. "Need I remind you, Rachel, that legally we're still considered man and wife. Therefore, I happen to think that who your friends are is still my damned business.''

"That sounds like a threat," Rachel retorted, her own sarcasm gaining ground. She thoroughly disliked this conversation and the direction it was taking. They had just found their missing son, for heaven's sake. It was time to let bygones be bygones—for a while—and just be happy. But it was as if finding that one single beer in her refrigerator had somehow sent Ross racing down a one-way alley marked Tunnel Vision.

"Look," Ross said. "Someone obviously purchased that beer and I'd like to know who that person was.''

"I would tell you, Ross, if I knew," Rachel snapped.

"Well, actually, the fact that you're trying your best to hide the truth from me, tells me plenty.''

"I've never heard you say anything so ridiculous in your life, Ross."

"Who's the guy?"

"What?"

Suddenly, running his fingers through his hair, Ross stepped back, turned and then walked to the window to gaze out momentarily. Obviously, he decided, it was time he did something to regain his equilibrium before he lost it for good. He knew it was crazy and downright out of line for him to be so worked up over a bottle of beer he'd found in Rachel's refrigerator, but, hell, he was. Big-time. Just the thought of some other man—friend or boyfriend—sitting at her kitchen table, sipping on a cold beer while chatting with her, ate holes in his gut the size of golf balls. She'd never offered him a damned beer whenever he'd come to visit his kids since they'd been separated. In truth, he'd never been a jealous man before, but right this minute, he damned sure was.

Rachel gaped at him. "What did you mean by that?"

Ross intended to soften his tone of voice, but for some reason he couldn't bring himself to do it. "I think you know exactly what I mean."

Taking a deep breath, Rachel glared at him. "Ross, let's get something straight right here and now. First of all, this is my house. My friends—male or female—who come and go through here are my business, not yours. And, secondly, I personally could care less who left that dumb beer in my refrigerator, so why is it such a major concern for you?" Then, suddenly, she cocked her head to one side and gave a slight smirk. "Ross, are you trying to imply that you think I'm seeing another man?"

Ross's gut knotted. In one split second his eyes darkened to the shade of black-brown. "Well, are you?" he growled as his heart pounded out the seconds that ticked by.

She gaped at him. "I can't believe that you'd think that of me."

"Really? Why not? You were, after all, the one who wanted out of our marriage, remember?"

"And I told you why I did."

"But did you tell me everything?" he said, strolling up to her with a serious look on his face.

Rachel's eyes widened. "I certainly don't have to take this kind of nonsense sitting down. Not when I recall all the times that you came home late and said it was business that kept you. I believed you. But maybe I shouldn't have. After all, was it really business?"

Now it was Ross's turn to gape at her. "I never cheated on you, Rachel. Never," he exclaimed defensively. "Nor am I doing so now."

"Well, neither am I," Rachel retorted.

"Well, good," Ross replied, once again taking a step back and using the moment to regain his cool. "I'm glad to know that we're both playing by the rules."

"Yes," she agreed. "So am I."

Suddenly Rachel heard her sister clear her throat loudly. She turned in that direction and saw Jan in the doorway.

"Look," Jan said. "I can shed some light on the mystery beer Ross found in your refrigerator."

"That isn't necessary, Jan," Rachel replied, sharply. Too sharply. She was allowing her frustration with the moment to get to her.

"I'm interested in what you have to say," Ross said, coming to stand at the middle of the room with his feet spread apart and his hands planted determinedly on his hips. He leveled his gaze on Jan's face.

"Well," Jan said, giving her lips a nervous lick, "it belonged to my ex-boyfriend. We came over here one night and he brought a six-pack of beer along with him. I remember because I was the one who put it in Rachel's refrigerator for him."

"I see," Ross replied.

Jan clapped her hands together. "So, now, that should explain everything," she said, brightly.

But the moment she stopped speaking, the silence that followed still sizzled with unresolved tension.

Jan cleared her throat again. "I'm going home now," she said a moment later. "See you all in the morning, okay?"

"Thanks, Jan, for everything you did today," Rachel replied as she followed her sister out the front door.

By the time Rachel returned to the kitchen, her desire to argue had disappeared and she and Ross sat down at opposite ends of the kitchen table to eat in silence. When Rachel was done, she excused herself and went to see about the boys, finding them sound asleep in their beds, just as she had expected them to be. Still, after the trauma of today, it did her heart good to check on them. Jorgie's feet were sticking out from under the sheet that covered him, so Rachel tucked it under the foot of his mattress. Danny was covered up to his chin and was sweating, so she loosed the sheet around him so he wouldn't be so warm. Then she stepped back and thought—really thought—of today's events.

Suddenly the emotions that she had held in check came crashing in like a huge tidal wave against a faulty seawall that had no means of holding back the flood. As she shoved Danny's bangs back from his forehead, and then Jorgie's, tears slipped relentlessly down her face.

A moment later she felt certain that someone—Ross, undoubtedly—was watching her. Glancing back over her shoulder, she saw him standing in the doorway, his hands braced on each side of the framework. His white dress shirt was pulled out of his trousers and unbuttoned all the way down the front. "Mind if I shower?" he asked.

Rachel's mouth went dry at the sight of him and she gaped at the dark, springing hair trailing downward through the opening in his shirt. Even at his absolute worst, Ross Murdock was a man to die for. So when at his absolute best—like now—half undressed and almost savage-looking in his sex appeal, he was indescribable. It had been more than six months since she'd run her fingers through that hair on his chest. She swallowed hard and quickly wiped at her tears. "Uh, you can use the bath just down the hall."

Frowning at her, Ross immediately dropped his arms to his sides and stepped into the bedroom. "Hey, are you crying?" he asked, studying her features more carefully. Finally he caught her chin and turned her face so that the light from the hallway would give him a better look.

"I'm okay," she quickly remarked, trying her best to erase any signs of moisture on her cheeks. She hated for anyone to see her cry. Most especially, Ross. Her father had always told her that men didn't love women who were crybabies. Unfortunately, his cruelly spoken words had left a lasting impression on the child she had been at the time. Actually, they'd left a deep scar on the adult she was today. She had loved her father with all of her heart and had done everything within her power to win his love in return. But she'd finally come to realize that he didn't care about her. Her own father hadn't even cared. At least he'd taught her an extraordinary lesson about men and how to survive, in spite of any emotional neglect she might suffer at their hands. Goodness knows, she'd learned to survive his. And now she was learning to survive Ross's.

But unfortunately, for the moment, anyway, it seemed she wasn't doing such a fantastic job of surviving anything and tears began to slip down her face once again, regardless of her efforts to prevent them. Wanting to get past Ross before he noticed she was crying, Rachel dropped her eyes to the floor and started from the room.

Ross immediately stepped into her path. "Come here, Rachel," he whispered, pulling her into his arms. "And for heaven's sake, don't fight me on this. What can it possibly hurt if I hold you for a moment?"

If he only knew, Rachel thought to herself as her heart lodged in her chest like a heavy boulder.

Still, in spite of her feelings on the matter, she didn't fight Ross as his strong arms closed around her. He smelled of spicy cologne and the humid outdoors, of sweat and dust.

Actually, though, what impressed her the most was his hard, fit body, and Rachel couldn't help but remember how well she knew every solid, sexy inch of him. And if she hadn't had her emotional guards up, she would have recognized his embrace as the one place in all the world where she felt safe. As it was, she was more concerned with keeping her pride and not letting him see that she still needed him. Because, in truth, it wouldn't have done either of them a bit of good.

Ross gazed into her face. "Are you sure you're okay?"

Actually, in that moment Rachel wasn't sure of anything, except one undeniable fact. No matter how much she wanted to convince herself otherwise, she still yearned for this man to hold her—and to want her—and to make love to her as much today as she ever had.

Which, given any serious thought at all, only went to prove how stupid she obviously was after the way he'd treated her in the last years of their marriage and how much she needed to keep her weak little self as far away from him as possible.

Keeping that thought utmost in her mind, Rachel nodded and after quickly scooting past him, headed down the hall for the kitchen. A few moments later she heard the door to the hall bath close and knew that Ross had gone to take his shower. She covered the leftover food and placed it in the refrigerator. By the time she'd finished cleaning the kitchen table, Ross had emerged from the bathroom, wearing only the black tuxedo trousers and a white towel around his neck. His straight dark hair was damp and hung loosely across his forehead. As a result, Rachel's stomach did a somersault. Even his feet were bare—which suddenly made the whole scene in front of her seem far too homey and much too intimate for her own good. It was definitely time for him to leave for the night.

"Well," Rachel exclaimed, dragging in a deep, uneven breath, "I guess it's my turn to get cleaned up for bed."

For some reason her words seemed to hang in midair. Either that, or she was just getting so tired that her thought processes were slowing down. She wanted to call it a night, but frankly, with Ross standing there, half naked and looking expectant of something— though she wasn't sure of what—she didn't know quite how to go about it. So she whirled around and headed down the hallway. "Ross, I'm exhausted. I'm going to take my shower now and then head straight to bed for the night. So, if you don't mind, would you please just lock up as you leave?''

Rachel heard when he cleared his throat, and for some reason her heart stopped momentarily, as did her movement down the hall. "Um . . . Rachel?"

Hesitating with a growing fear that she knew what he was going to say, she finally turned slowly to face him. "What?" By now her heart was pounding erratically.

Ross scratched the top of his head as though in a deep concentration. "Look, I, uh . . ."

Rachel had no earthly idea what he was having so much difficulty in saying to her, and yet she had this strange feeling that she knew exactly what it was.

Grinning at her sheepishly, Ross grabbed hold of the ends of the towel hanging around his neck, planted his bare feet apart and then widened his grin just a fraction more. "Well, actually, Rachel, here's the deal. I was hoping I could sleep here tonight."

Rachel's mouth dropped open. "I'm sorry," she said calmly, but her insides had tightened and were presently vibrating like the strings of a guitar in spite of her efforts to remain as cool as possible. "Would you mind repeating that for me?"

"I said, I was hoping that you wouldn't mind so much if I slept over tonight. It's so late and all . . . Besides, the sofa looks comfortable enough to suit me."

Rachel brought her fingers to the center of her chest. "My sofa?" she exclaimed. "You intend to sleep on my sofa tonight?"

Again, he scratched the top of his head in a way that implied he was trying real hard to think of just the right thing to say to her. "Look, I've had my rabies shot. I don't have any claws, and I don't need a litter box. Oh, and I promise not to keep you awake by howling at the moon. In fact, I'll be as quiet as a mouse and as incognito as that bottle of beer I found in your refrigerator. So, what do you say?"

The mention of that beer again caused Rachel's insides to cringe momentarily, but finally she regained her control and shook her head. "No way, Ross. We're separated, remember?"

He sighed heavily. "What does that have to do with me spending the rest of tonight over here? I already said I'll sleep on the sofa."

She ignored his comment. "Go to a motel."

"It could take me half the night to find a room. I'm too tired."

"How can you say that when you haven't even tried to find one?"

"I don't have a car, remember?"

"Oh . . . yeah," Rachel replied. She'd forgotten about that one little detail. *She could let him have hers . . . But what if she ended up needing it during the night?* "I'll call you a cab."

"Look, Rachel," Ross replied, running frustrated fingers through his hair, "why can't we just keep this simple for tonight?" He settled his hands on his lean hips. "Besides, it's already after midnight. We're both exhausted. I'm without a car. And I don't even have an extra change of clothes with me. I can assure you that I wouldn't send you out into the cold night like this."

"It's warm outside," Rachel replied.

"That's not my point, and you know it," he drawled insistently. "Look, all I need right now is some sleep."

He sounded almost as worn out as she felt, Rachel thought. Almost. And, in truth, he had come all this way and it had been a long emotional night for both of them. And he was right. He wouldn't have made her leave in the dead of night—not under any circumstances. Besides, what harm could it do to allow him to stay here for the few hours that remained until daybreak?

Plenty, actually, she told herself. Especially if she wasn't careful. But she would be. She would be *very* careful.

"Rachel?" Ross said. She couldn't help herself; she glanced back at him and saw a kind of pleading look in his eyes that tore at her heart. "Please . . . Rachel."

Suddenly, Rachel remembered that it was his birthday and she felt so guilty and insensitive in that moment that she would've probably given in to any request from him.

"Oh—all right," she said, barely above a whisper. Then she intentionally marched herself halfway down the hall toward her bedroom before stopping and glancing back at him from over her shoulder. "In that case, it would be ridiculous of you to sleep on the sofa when there's a spare bedroom. Just don't get any crazy ideas of trying to make this into some kind of habit."

"Now would I do something like that?" he asked innocently.

"A-and I know it's past midnight now, but happy birthday, anyway," she stammered awkwardly before strutting the rest of the way down the hall to her bedroom. Entering, she closed the door behind her and turned the lock.

And then, finally alone, she sat on the edge of her bed and had herself a good cry.

* * *

Rachel couldn't sleep. She was hot. Then she was cold. Her skin burned. Then it itched. She scratched, and then she rubbed. But nothing helped. Sometimes it felt as though she was sleeping on a bed of fire ants.

Damn Ross, anyway. This was all his fault. He didn't have to sleep at her house. There were motels nearby. In fact, there were plenty in Lafayette, just twenty miles away. A taxi could've driven him to the nearest one in no time at all.

Heaven help her, but she'd been unable to resist noticing how gorgeously tempting he'd looked without his shirt tonight. One glance at any part of his naked anatomy had always been enough to turn her on. But, for heaven's sake, this time it had left her boiling, and no matter how hard she tried, she couldn't stop thinking of him. Not even for one single second. She was hot. She was frustrated. And she was angry with herself for being so vulnerable. So needy. Ross was probably sound asleep—in the nude, of course. He always slept naked.

And just that thought alone was driving her crazy. She was burning up and didn't think that she could take much more heat without exploding into a million tiny pieces. Already, the inside of her mouth was as dry as a border town during a Texas drought.

Turning over in her bed Rachel closed her eyes tight and prayed for sleep to overcome her. But after several more minutes she finally resolved that it wasn't going to happen. Not without some kind of relief from this need building inside her.

Finally, sighing in defeat, she sat up, then planted her feet on the floor. Stalling for several moments, she debated with her common sense before finally taking a deep, decisive breath to go ahead with this suddenly crazy idea of hers.

Leaving the safety of her bedroom, she walked down the hall and knocked lightly on the door to the spare bedroom. When she received no reply, she knocked again and then opened the door just enough to peek inside. "Ross, are you asleep?"

Rachel heard the rustling of sheets as he rolled over in bed and clicked on the bedside lamp. "Rachel? What's wrong?"

"Nothing," she said quickly. "I, uh... Do you mind if I come in?"

Looking somewhat surprised by her request, he paused momentarily. "Why, no. Not at all." He yawned as he glanced at the clock near the lamp. "Jeez, it's almost three o'clock in the morning."

"I—I know," Rachel said softly, quietly shutting the bedroom door behind her. The last thing she wanted was for their voices to carry across the hallway and awaken the boys. "I couldn't sleep, and so I thought that...well, I guess I just didn't want to be alone tonight... Anyway, I thought that maybe we could talk for a while."

Ross rubbed one eye with the back of his hand. "Talk? You want to talk right now, at this time of night?" he asked incredulously. Immediately sitting up in bed, he leaned back against the solid oak headboard and then placed his hands behind his head.

Rachel grimaced. "I know my timing is bad, but—"

Narrowing his eyes, Ross studied her momentarily. "I guess that all depends on what you want to talk about."

Rachel swallowed. This wasn't getting any easier for her. Which was so ridiculous, considering she'd already shared ten years of marriage with this man. Still, her insides were trembling and she felt breathless...almost dizzy with anxiety. She had no idea what had possessed her to cross the line that she'd previously drawn between them. Obviously she had been more affected by Danny's disappearance today than she'd originally thought. What else could explain this unusual behavior in her?

She'd undoubtedly lost her mind, Rachel told herself a moment later, and now was as good a time as any to back away before it was too late for her to make a beeline back to her own bedroom. "I, uh... Look, I really don't know why I came in here. Just forget that I ever did, okay?" she said, attempting to turn away from him at that point. But Ross closed his fingers around her forearm and pulled her down to a sitting position on the edge of the mattress.

"Now wait just a minute, Rachel," he said gently, almost understandingly so. "Look, I can see that this isn't easy for you to have to do all by yourself, so I'm going to help, okay?" Then without waiting for her reply, he smiled, took her hand and placed it over his maleness. "Is this what you came in here for?"

It was already too late.

Shock rippled through Rachel as her heart began to pound in her ears. Ross was hard—and hot—even through the sheet covering his body, and he grew even harder as her hand closed around him. His entire body tensed and for the first time since entering the spare bedroom where he'd lain asleep, Rachel felt a moment of triumph. It had been a long time since she had held him in such a way and it felt deliciously wicked. "Yes," she finally replied, barely above a whisper.

Something hot and potent flickered to life in the depths of Ross's dark, brooding eyes. With still a hint of a smile on his lips, he pulled back the sheet on the bed and said, "In that case, care to join me?"

Rachel's breath locked in her throat. He was naked—and absolutely gorgeous—just as she had thought he would be.

With pulses racing, Rachel watched him watch her stand, slip her thigh-length cotton nightshirt over her head and then let it drop to the floor. Now she was completely naked to his viewing.

Ross groaned. "I take it, your answer's yes."

Rachel smiled.

Before she could even climb into bed with him, he reached out and pulled her down on top of him. Their mouths were now mere inches apart, and they stared into each other's eyes for one timeless moment.

Then Ross's hand tangled itself in the back of her hair. His other hand came to rest at her waist and he eased her into the exact position he liked best. "Kiss me, Rachel," he said. "With your mouth open."

Dazzled by her own growing need to have him, Rachel immediately obeyed and kissed him in the way he instructed. In no time at all he was using his hands, his tongue, his whole body, as an instrument for giving her the most divine pleasure she'd ever known, and she eventually exploded in a climax, not only once, but over and over again until she was drenched in perspiration and completely exhausted.

And then, at last, with his arms around her, she was granted her earlier wish and fell into a deep, restful sleep.

* * *

Rachel was startled awake by a growing sense that something wasn't quite right with her surroundings. Now, however, fully conscious, she lay motionless and stared at the ceiling overhead. When the naked body lying next to her moved slightly and she felt the immediate rush of cold air where once hot flesh had pressed against her side, she was stunned into realizing that she was naked, too. Immediately her breath locked in her throat and a hot sensation gushed through her body, making sure she received a good dose of morning reality. Like harvested grain funneling into a silo, the memory of what she and Ross had done together last night came pouring in, and within a second she felt even more naked than she had in a long, long time.

She had weakened. She couldn't believe that she had done so, but it was true. She had. The evidence was too overwhelming for her to try to deny. The memories themselves were much too vivid. She was nude. He was nude. The sheets on the bed were a tangled mess. Her lips were swollen—a result, she knew, of Ross's ardent kisses. And the images in her mind of what they done together... Well, they were simply too real to have been a dream.

It was a rather rude awakening for someone who had promised herself to stay in control, not to mention a rather bad start on a new day. But it was all her own fault. She'd gotten what she'd come looking for last night, and more. In fact, much more. Ross—damn him for being such a passionate lover—had made sure of that.

Regardless, though, she'd made a mistake. A big mistake. Having sex with Ross last night hadn't solved any of their problems. In fact, now, in the light of dawn, it was easy to see that her reckless behavior was undoubtedly going to have an adverse effect on their already strained relationship. She was never going to be so impetuous and so foolish again. Never.

The whole problem with her and Ross was that they hadn't just shared a night of intense sex. The kind that they could've simply gotten out of bed this morning and walked away from without suffering any ill effects. Oh, no... not them. That would've been too easy. Instead they'd shared something—a sensuous oneness, she supposed—that had always been a part of their lovemaking. Obviously, after what they'd just shared a few hours ago, it still was. And, because of that, Ross was liable to think she still cared for him, when in fact that was the very last thing she wanted him to think. It had taken her years to face the truth of where her marriage was heading. But once she'd realized that she and the kids were no longer an important ingredient for Ross's happiness, she hadn't waited around for him to finally abandon them.

And now that she'd had the courage to take that step, she couldn't let herself fall into the same trap her mother had. She couldn't let Ross come back into her life in that way again. Not now.

Not ever.

Chapter Four

Having made a decision, Rachel knew it was time for her to get out of bed before Ross awoke. Anticipating her next move, she swallowed hard and watched the steady rhythm of his constant breathing. Using caution, she moved her arm away from him ever so slightly, then held her breath and waited to see his response. When there wasn't any, she quickly eased off the edge of the bed, scooped up her cotton T-shirt from the floor and slipped it on over her head. With pulse racing and her eyes still glued on Ross for any sign that she might have awakened him, she moved silently toward the door.

Within a matter of seconds she was out of the spare bedroom and heading down the hall to her bath. She climbed in the shower for a long, leisurely cleansing in the hopes that when she was done, she could wash away the evidence and the memories of last night's lovemaking. But, unfortunately, she soon realized that it didn't work. All the visible evidence of their love-making had been washed away, but the memories . . . well, they still lingered on.

She dressed quickly in a pair of white denim shorts and a lime-green tank top. Entering the kitchen, she made a pot of coffee, then, after it was brewed, sat down on the deacon's bench under the kitchen window with a cupful in one hand.

So much had happened to her in the past twenty-four hours, it seemed hard to believe that just yesterday morning her life had been almost normal. Almost like that of a regular person. Now, it was turned upside down, again. If only she didn't have to face Ross today. Certainly, that alone would have removed some of the pressure she was feeling.

But, needless to say, short of her running away from home, she seemed to have little choice in the matter. Turning, she propped her feet up on the benchseat and stared out the window in the hopes of stumbling upon an idea that would allow her to escape the confrontation that she knew was inevitable. But instead of finding a way to rescue herself, she unconsciously became enthralled with the invading thoughts of those rare, bittersweet moments that she'd spent in Ross's arms last night.

Ross awakened with a start and knew instinctively that Rachel had already left the bed where he lay. Quickly, feeling his way across the area of the mattress right next to him, he confirmed his suspicions in less than a second.

In truth, he should've known that she would be gone when he awoke. Staying would have been asking too much of her. Lately, Rachel acted more like an elusive fluttering little bird. She wanted to believe that her heart and soul were free—that they didn't belong to anyone anymore. But she was wrong. Every single cell in her body belonged to him. And his belonged to her. It wasn't even his choice—or, hers, for that matter. Destiny had mated them for life, and it was pointless of her—or anyone—to try to sever the bond.

Lying on his back and recalling what he and Rachel had done together last night, Ross finally rolled over onto his side and grinned to himself. Heaven help them both, but what a night they'd had together! A night of some rather wild and unexpected sex. In fact, even after the many times he'd taken her over the edge, he was mildly surprised to discover that his hunger for her right then was still as great as it had been when she'd come knocking on the spare bedroom door. In truth, last night's sex had been the best ever. And what made it even more pleasurable for him to think about now was that it had all been Rachel's idea.

She'd been wild—wicked, in fact—in her mission to seduce him. She had used her tongue, her mouth, her entire body, to deliberately drive him beyond control. Both of them had had an intense, driving need that had inevitably exploded over and over again, in a passionate climax. It was perfectly clear to him now that Rachel still wanted him. She had, after all, come to *him* last night. And that in itself pleased him greatly. Maybe winning her back wasn't going to be as difficult as he had originally thought.

With that in mind, and a smile on his face to match the sincere, good feeling inside of him, he climbed out of bed and slipped on his briefs. Opening the spare bedroom door and smelling the aroma of freshly brewed coffee drifting through the air, he plodded down the hall toward the kitchen to find his wife. He looked for her at every corner and turn and finally found her seated on a bench under the kitchen window, sipping on what he presumed was her first cup of coffee. Pausing in the doorway for a second more, he allowed himself the pleasure of watching her without her being aware yet of his presence. He couldn't wait to touch her again. And to take her once more as his very own. Last night her body had been so ready and willing to accept his...

It made him hot all over again just to think about it.

And yet... there was something about her manner this morning that was keeping him at bay. Something—her straight, rigid spine, perhaps—that told him to tread carefully through the deep tension that he now sensed was somehow separating them once more. "Good morning," he said after carefully contemplating what his next move should be.

Rachel was lost in her own thoughts and jarred at the sound of Ross's voice. Not that she wasn't expecting to hear it, sooner or later. Nonetheless, she was still shaken by the deep tenor and sloshed coffee over the rim of her cup. The warm liquid splattered across her hand and ended up spilling on her otherwise clean white ceramic tile floor. But, for now, she chose to ignore the mess it made. After all, she had more important matters to consider. She was just thankful that the coffee in her cup was no longer piping hot.

Taking a deep breath, she turned slightly in her seat, only enough, in fact, to see that Ross was standing in the doorway. Just as she had feared, at the sight of him, her stomach went kerplunk.

Bare-chested—with only a pair of black cotton briefs covering his manhood, Ross wore a smile on his face as wide as the Mississippi River. Rachel couldn't help herself as he began to stroll toward her. Force of habit—or perhaps it was more a force of nature—she gawked at the fitness of his lean, hard body and at the pure, male sexuality that emanated from his every pore. She fixed her wide, fascinated gaze on the trail of dark, curly hair that started at the center of his chest, traveled down his abdomen and disappeared beneath the waistband of his briefs. The briefs themselves encircled his waist just a fraction below his navel.

Rachel recalled how last night her tongue had followed that same dark, curly trail down his body—only he hadn't been wearing his briefs—but then again, she hadn't bothered to stop just below his waistline, either. Even now, the vivid memory of her conduct last night was enough to leave her breathless. In truth, after today, if it continued to haunt her as viciously as now, she was going to have a hard time living with herself. What she really needed more than anything was a good old-fashioned memory lapse.

"I wondered where you'd gone off to," Ross said, seemingly undaunted by her silence. "Then I opened the bedroom door and smelled fresh coffee. And as you well know, kitten, other than you, there's nothing more I'd rather have first thing in the morning than a good cup of coffee."

Rachel groaned to herself. She could tell already that this wasn't going to be one of her days. "Help yourself. It's just brewed," she replied, carefully guarding herself against reacting to his last remark. *First thing in the morning, indeed.* Instead, she turned back and gazed once more out the window. She knew, however, that he was watching her the entire time because she could feel a kind of heat on her neck.

"You don't seem very talkative this morning," he remarked. "After last night, I thought that you'd have plenty to say."

"The weather looks gloomy."

"Really?" he replied, walking up closer to the window to peer out. "I hadn't noticed yet." He leaned over her shoulder. "Yeah. It's sort of cloudy, all right. Kind of like in here, don't you think?"

Without looking back at him, Rachel mumbled, "I guess so."

Ross stepped away, but Rachel could still feel his eyes on her back. "So what's the deal, Rachel?" he asked a moment later. "Why is it that you can't seem to turn around and look at me?"

"Maybe I would, if you were dressed properly," she remarked. "Hasn't it occurred to you that the kids could wake up at any minute?"

"The kids are sound asleep—and probably will be for quite a while yet."

"Sometimes they wake up early."

"Well, in that case, don't you think that they've seen me in my underwear before? I'm their father, for heaven's sake."

Of course, the kids had seen him in his underwear, Rachel thought to herself. And so had she. Plenty of times. Too many times to ever forget what he looked like when barely dressed. She'd seen him naked, too. And that was the real problem. She'd seen him nude too recently to be able to think straight now.

"You know," he stated a moment later, "my lack of clothing last night didn't seem to bother you in the least."

She had known he would do this to her. "That was last night—and a different case, altogether. Besides, it was dark."

"Not in my room, it wasn't. The light was on the majority of the time, remember?"

In truth, she would never forget it.

She glanced at Ross and saw that he seemed amused at her embarrassment. "Come on, Rachel," he said, "turn yourself completely around. We need to talk."

Still deliberately gazing out the window for lack of something better to do in that moment, Rachel shook her head. "There's nothing more for us to talk about, Ross. We've already said it all."

"Oh, but I think there's still plenty for us to talk about. For starters, there's the passion that we shared last night. I don't know about you, but I was pretty impressed by it all."

Pulling up her emotional guards, Rachel stiffened her spine. "Look, what happened, happened, okay? But it's over with. So let's just put it behind us and go on."

Ross smirked. "You're kidding me. You could actually do that after last night?" he asked.

Rachel took a deep, steadying breath. "Of course."

Ross came around so that he faced her and then plopped down on that end of the deacon's bench. "Well, I can't, and I happen to believe that you can't, either."

"Why not? Don't you think it's possible for me to have a one-night fling?"

"Rachel, honey," he said as he leaned in closer to her with a sudden grin on his face. Just the fact that he was half naked and sitting so close was enough to rattle her good. She had the sudden urge to dig her fingers into his chest muscles, but she knew that to touch him in any fashion at the moment would be her undoing. "What we shared last night was no one-night fling, and you know it," Ross continued. "That was some of the best sex we've ever had."

Rachel took another deep breath. "So I weakened all of a sudden and you accommodated me. So, what?"

Ross gaped at her. "Accommodated you? That's ridiculous. I wanted you as much as you wanted me. We accommodated each other, and quite well, I might add."

"Nevertheless," she said prudently, "last night meant nothing. One night of some rather rambunctious sex has never been enough for any couple to build a lasting relationship on. Not even one they're trying to rebuild."

"I agree with that. But you're wrong about us, Rachel. What we shared last night came from need— from in here," he said, gesturing toward his gut. "And so far it's managed to survive through ten years of marriage between our two strikingly different personalities."

Rachel couldn't handle much more of this. Sighing, she turned to face him. "Ross?"

"Yeah?"

She held up her chin at a distinct angle. "Look, I hate to seem ungracious and all... But I think it's best now if you call yourself a cab and go to a hotel before the kids wake up."

Getting up slowly from his end of the deacon's bench, suddenly Ross's expression went blank. "Is that a fact?"

She nodded. "Yes, it is."

"Then I guess you were right. Last night didn't change anything for you."

"No," Rachel replied. "Did you think it would?"

One corner of Ross's mouth lifted in a smirk. "That would've been rather foolish of me, now wouldn't it?"

"I'm sorry, Ross. Really, I am."

"Yeah, well . . ."

Rachel saw anger flash across his eyes.

He ran his fingers through his hair. "Well, in that case," he said, obviously shutting himself off from her, "would you mind if I had a cup of coffee before I leave?"

Frowning, Rachel glanced back at the full pot she'd made earlier. "No, of course not. Help yourself."

Expecting him to go straight for a cup of coffee, Rachel rose and politely stepped to the side so that he could pass. But instead, he surprised her by suddenly turning and trapping her in a corner. Startled, Rachel immediately sucked in a breath and then held on to it for dear life. "What? What are you doing?" she finally gasped.

"Look, Rachel, you're angry with me right now and I can understand that. But you can't just throw ten years of our lives down the drain. Not without giving me another chance."

The depth of emotion in his voice caused Rachel's heart to flutter around in her chest like some silly little butterfly who'd just found its wings. Regardless, this was one time she wasn't going to let herself fall under his spell. "Let me pass, Ross."

"Look," he said, ignoring her request, "I made some mistakes in our marriage. I know that now. But I'm a changed man."

"Jeez..." she said, shaking her head slowly, "I wonder just how many times I heard my father say something like that to my mother. The problem was, he never meant it. And I don't think that you do, either. Remember," she quipped, "I know how this game works. You're just telling me what you think I want to hear. But it's not because you want me back. It's because you can't stand the idea that I walked out on you first."

"That's not true, Rachel. And I'm not your father. So, it isn't fair of you to compare us."

"Well, I'm not going to be my mother, that's for sure. Not if I can help it, anyway."

Ross dropped his arms to his sides and gazed at her long and hard. "Look, Rachel, I'm not going to sit back and let you end this marriage unless you have a good, solid reason for it. And, frankly, my dear, so far you haven't given me one."

Inhaling deeply, Rachel gathered up all of her courage. In truth, Ross had simply come too close to realizing the truth about her. No one, absolutely no one, needed to know how scared she was of being hurt, again—so hurt, in fact, that she feared a recovery in this lifetime would be impossible for her. She gave him a haughty look. "Ross, you have every right to do as you see fit, but I'm telling you right now, it won't do any good."

Ross's features hardened. "It looks to me like you've already made up your mind about us."

"Yes, you're right. I have," Rachel replied, holding up her emotional armor against him.

He gave her a compliant yet somewhat cocky grin. "Well, in that case," he said, "so have I."

Whirling around, he headed out of the kitchen. Reaching the doorway leading into the living room, he turned and targeted her with a level glare. "I'll be back, Rachel. You can count on it."

A moment later he lifted the receiver to the telephone in the living room, called himself a cab and, by the time he'd dressed it had arrived and Ross walked right out her front door without uttering another word.

A few days later Ross sat behind the desk in his office. Across from him was Christian Chandler, his attorney and closest friend.

"You can't be serious about this," Christian said.

"Indeed, I am," Ross replied adamantly.

"Look, I know you want to work things out with Rachel, but don't you think this move is a bit drastic?"

"Not in this day and age. With today's modern technology, I can set up an office anywhere in the world and still have all the information I need at my fingertips."

Christian shook his head. "I know that, Ross. But to move your office to Abbeville, Louisiana. Let's face it. It's not exactly the business empire of the world."

"Look, I'm not moving the whole office. Just myself. Everyone else is staying here."

Once again, Christian shook his head. "This is crazy, Ross, even for you."

Ross laughed meaningfully. "Look, Rachel doesn't believe that I'm capable of placing my family before my career. And up until the night that Danny turned up missing, I guess I didn't think so, either. But today I happen to know otherwise. Rachel and the kids are positively and absolutely everything to me. *Everything,*" he emphasized.

Christian held up his hands in surrender. "Hey, I'm convinced."

Ross sat back in his chair and sighed. "Look, I'm sorry. I don't mean to take this out on you. It's just . . . well, I'm not myself these days."

"I'll say," Christian mumbled. "Rachel's being a tough cookie, is she?"

Ross crossed his arms over his chest. "Actually, she's being downright stubborn."

Grinning, Christian stood to leave. "Keep your chin up, partner. Eventually she's bound to see things your way."

"How can you be so sure?" Ross asked.

"Because I happen to remember the passion the two of you once had for one another. That kind of feeling doesn't just go away. Not ever. No matter what."

Ross leaned forward and placed his arms on his desk. "Christian, you have positively no idea how much I'm counting on that being the absolute truth."

Sitting in a lounge chair in her backyard, Rachel watched her sons as they played. It had been a little more than two weeks now since the ordeal with Danny and Orlan, but still she found it difficult to allow either of her sons out of her sight for any length of time. Today, when they'd said that they wanted to go outside, she'd poured herself a glass of ice tea, slipped on her sunshades and followed.

Realizing, however, that it was now time for lunch, Rachel got up from her chair on the patio and instructed her two children to go inside and wash their hands. While they were in the bathroom, she prepared one of their favorite noontime meals, peanut butter and jelly sandwiches, and then brought their plates outside to the picnic table. A few minutes later they were back, sitting at the table, one on either side of her. They were all busy eating when Jorgie looked up and said, "Mommy, when's Daddy coming back to see us? I miss him sometimes."

"Me, too," Danny chimed in, chewing on a bite of his sandwich. He had strawberry jelly at both corners of his mouth when Rachel glanced down at him.

Stunned, Rachel drew in an immediate breath. "I, uh, I don't know," she replied, flicking her eyes from one child to the other. "He didn't say when he left."

"How come he didn't say goodbye?" Jorgie asked.

"I told you, Jorgie. Something very disturbing came up and he had to leave in a hurry. But he kissed you and Danny when he left, although you didn't know it because you were still asleep."

"Why didn't he wake me up? I wanted him to."

"Because he knew that you were tired."

"Can Daddy come live with us again?" Danny asked from out of the blue.

Rachel's breath froze in her throat and she didn't think that she'd be able to swallow another bite of food. Finally, though, she pulled herself together and turned her head in his direction. "I—I don't think so, Danny."

"Why not?" he asked innocently as only a five-year-old could while at the same time trying to drink from a glass of milk. But a moment later he set his glass down, looked her square in the face, and waited for an answer.

An answer she wasn't really prepared to give him at the moment.

An enormous lump in her throat constricted her ability to breathe normally.

If there was one single thing that Rachel hated about her decision to separate her sons from their father, it was the hurt she had known it would cause them. But she honestly believed that if she had lingered in her marriage, they would have eventually suffered even more. God knew, she had, when her father had finally abandoned them and her mother had fallen completely apart. Still, she knew her sons loved their father and needed him in their daily lives.

Jorgie took it upon himself to frown at his younger brother. "That's a dumb question, silly," he said. "Daddy can't come live with us."

"But why not?" Danny asked as his eyes widened in suspense.

Before Rachel could answer, Jorgie took charge once more of the conversation. "'Cause Mommy's still mad at him, that's why not," he explained.

The lump in Rachel's throat was now gone, but her heart and soul suddenly congregated in its place. "I'm not m-mad at Daddy," she stammered. "Well... I mean, I guess I am, in a way."

Danny drew his eyebrows together in much the same fashion as she'd often seen Ross do on so many occasions in the past. "When you stop being mad at Daddy, then can he come live with us?" he asked hopefully.

Sick to her stomach, Rachel shook her head slowly. "I'm sorry, Danny, but I can't promise you that."

Rachel knew that she was avoiding the truth, but now was clearly not the right time or place for such a difficult family discussion. Maybe her children didn't need preparation for it, but she certainly did.

And that, she told herself, was her only reason for edging around the truth. It had absolutely nothing to do with any doubts she may have concerning Ross.

Right?

Uh, r-right, her inner voice finally stammered after it was poked awake by one of her ribs.

Chapter Five

The next morning, at the first sign of daylight, Rachel rose, took a quick, wake-up shower, slipped on her short white silk robe and hurried into the kitchen to brew a pot of coffee. When it was done, she poured herself a cup, doctored it with a sugar substitute and took her first sip. As always, she was lured by the spray of bright morning sunlight coming through her kitchen window and sat down on the deacon's bench under it.

Last night she'd dreamed about Ross, again—about their reckless night of unbridled passion. The dream had seemed so breathtakingly real to her that when she had finally succeeded in pulling herself awake, she'd expected to turn over in her bed and see him sleeping beside her. And the truth of the matter was, she'd been mildly disappointed when she'd found that he wasn't. Well . . . maybe more than just mildly. Actually, her insides had cratered like a house of cards built upon a shaky table.

For Rachel, one of the hardest things for her to have to accept about her failed marriage was knowing that she hadn't been enough to make Ross happy. From the moment he'd kissed her for the first time, she had felt as though she'd found her nesting place in him, and she would have been content to have remained there forever had she been what he'd needed, as well. But over the years she'd been forced to realize that that wasn't the case. And now she knew her inability to please him was, in retrospect, the same kind of nasty dose of medicine that her mother had had to swallow all those years ago where her father was concerned. And it was those similarities that constantly fed Rachel's fear of being like her mother and loving a man so much that he had the power to destroy her.

Suddenly, Rachel heard sounds coming from the other end of the house. The sounds were little grunts and groans that led her to believe that her two sons were awake—which was just as well, she thought, considering that Jan had asked if she could pick them up to take them to the park for the day.

The grunts grew louder, as did the groans, and then all of a sudden Rachel heard a loud thud that made her think one of them might have fallen out of bed.

Actually, the boys had been more than active lately, especially since school had let out for summer vacation less than three weeks ago. Of course, she hadn't lost either of them in the past couple of weeks, thank goodness for that. And she felt certain that the local police department was grateful, too.

Scrambling to her feet, Rachel rushed off in the direction of her sons' bedroom. Her heart was pounding when she arrived in their doorway, until she saw what they were up to. Frowning, she placed her hands on her hips.

It wasn't that she minded the boys wrestling from time to time. She knew it was a game to them, but lately, sometimes the game simply got too rough. "Okay, break it up, guys," she said in a stern voice.

"It's not my fault," Danny replied the moment he looked up and saw his mother standing in the doorway. He was straddling his older brother—which made him look all the more guilty, in spite of his pleading of innocence. Pinning his older brother's arms above his head, Danny brazenly stated, "Jorgie started it."

"Did not," Jorgie countered.

"Did too," Danny replied.

Rachel stepped into the room. "Get off your brother this instant, Danny." He immediately followed her orders. "Now the two of you stand up." Danny rose first and then Jorgie got to his feet a moment later.

Danny pointed a finger toward Jorgie. "He hit me."

"You hit me first," Jorgie argued back.

"Why did you hit him first, Danny?" Rachel asked, keeping her voice level and unemotional.

Danny gave her a disgruntled shrug. "I don't know."

"He hit me 'cause he wanted my snake and I wouldn't give it to him, that's why," Jorgie said, his bottom lip trembling in anger. "And I'm not going to give it to him, either. No matter what."

Rachel's first thought was that Jorgie's anger was so unlike him. But then his words began to register. "Snake?" she echoed, hoping she had misunderstood him. "You don't have a snake, Jorgie."

"I do now," he replied, proudly straightening his small shoulders.

"And it's for real, too," Danny cut in.

"What do you mean, it's for real?"

"It's not a toy," Jorgie explained. "It's real, all right. My friend Kurt gave it to me yesterday." Then he turned, marched over to his bed and made a big production of lifting up an empty quart jar. "See?" he said. "It was in here."

Rachel felt her chest cave in. "And where is it now?"

"Right here," Jorgie replied, dropping the empty jar on his mattress and turning toward the bottom half of an old shoe box that was lying on the floor, pushed halfway under his bed. He pulled it out, peeked inside and then hesitated momentarily before saying, "Uh-oh, it's not here anymore."

Rachel scrambled to his side. "What do you mean, it's not here?" Hesitating for only a moment, she reached down, took the empty box from him and flipped it over to examine the bottom as though she might be lucky enough to have found the impetuous little snake somehow clinging to the cardboard underside. But the snake wasn't there, either. "Where is it, then?" she asked, her voice beginning to sound shrill, even to her own ears.

Jorgie shrugged his shoulders. "I don't know."

She whirled around to Danny. "Danny, do you have the snake?"

His eyes widened twice the size of normal. "Uh-uh," he said, shaking his head slowly. "I promise, Mommy, I don't have it."

Rachel turned back around, fearing she already knew the answer to her next question. ''Then where is it?''

The boys looked at each other, shrugged, and then at the same time said, ''I don't know.''

Rachel felt almost light-headed from the thought of having a snake missing in her house. Still, she bent over and cautiously examined under the lower bunk. After all, she had to do something. She couldn't just ignore the fact that a reptile was running loose in her house.

''It's not very big, Mommy,'' Jorgie said, proceeding to measure out about fifteen inches between his hands.

''Oh, God,'' Rachel murmured. She wasn't terrified of snakes, not like some people were. Still, she doubted if she could coexist in the same house with one. In fact, she was quite certain that one of them, either her or the snake, would have to go. Preferably, it would be the snake.

Oh, jeez . . . She didn't need this. Not today. Not after all that had been happening lately.

''It's just a nightcrawler,'' Danny chimed, in a teasing, get-even voice that Rachel knew was meant to intimidate his older brother. After all, now that the snake was lost, Danny was sharp enough to realize that Jorgie didn't have any proof that the snake wasn't just a big worm. It worked.

''It's not a nightcrawler, silly,'' Jorgie argued. ''It's a king snake. Kurt said so. And it's mine.''

''It's mine, too.''

''It is not.''

''Stop arguing,'' Rachel ordered. ''And help me look for it.''

"There it is," Jorgie squealed suddenly from somewhere behind her.

Rachel whirled around. "Where?"

"There," he said, pointing toward the closet. "It went in there."

Rachel's heart was pounding as she raced forward. She reminded herself that she wasn't really afraid of snakes. She just didn't like them. Period.

Without giving her mission any more thought than necessary—after all, she just might talk herself out of this altogether—Rachel tore into the bedroom closet, pulling out shoes and toys and boxes of goodness-knows-what-all from inside. She became so absorbed in trying to find the missing snake that she didn't realize the boys had wandered off to play in another room, or that her sister Jan had come inside the house after calling her name at the back door and getting no reply. When Rachel finally turned around, Jan was standing in the doorway of the bedroom with a scowl on her face. "What in the world are you doing?" she asked, cocking an eyebrow as she dropped her shoulder-strap purse to the floor and placed her hands on her hips. "Jeez, what a mess. Have you lost your mind, or something?"

"Oh, God, Jan, thank goodness, you're here," Rachel exclaimed, stepping over a pile of items in a desperate attempt to reach her sister. For a moment her eyes glistened with tears. So far, her frantic search hadn't turned up anything even closely resembling a living reptile. Or even a toy one, for that matter. She was really getting worried now that she might not be able to ever find it. "You see, there's this snake running loose," she said breathlessly.

Jan's expression changed drastically. "What snake?"

Rachel licked her lips anxiously. "Jorgie had this king snake in this jar and it got away—"

It was the wrong thing to have said in that moment, and Rachel knew it instantly. Her sister happened to be one of those people who *was* scared to death of snakes.

Jan froze. "It's loose? You mean . . . like it's crawling around somewhere in here? In this very room?" she asked, her voice barely above a whisper.

"Yes—but it's only a little snake, Jan. Hardly bigger than a worm. Jorgie said so himself. A-And I don't think it's poisonous. The problem is, it's somewhere in here, but I don't know where. You've got to help me find it."

Jan's face whitened. "Oh, God," she said, "I'm getting out of here."

"Wait! Jan, don't go," Rachel pleaded, trying to grab hold of her sister's hand, but Jan was quicker and wouldn't let her. "Please, Jan, I need your help. I can't find it alone."

Her sister paused in the doorway, but looked ready to run at the slightest provocation. "You can just forget it, Rachel. I'm not staying in here. I—I'm sorry. but you know that snakes and I just don't get along. This is one time you'll have to find someone else to help you."

"But it's just a little snake, Jan."

"Then why are you so upset?"

"I don't know," Rachel replied, her shoulders slumping in defeat. "I guess 'cause I can't find it."

Jan shivered. "I can't handle this, Rachel. I'm sorry."

Rachel realized in that moment that her sister wasn't going to be of any help to her. Jan's phobia had complete control of her. "Never mind. I understand," Rachel said.

"I'll take the boys out for breakfast."

Rachel nodded. "Thanks."

"Don't mention it," Jan said as she hurriedly scooped up her purse to leave. Stepping into the hallway, she called out to Jorgie and Danny, and they immediately came running to her side. A few minutes later Rachel watched through a window as Jan backed her red sports car out the drive and pulled away without even a backward glance toward the house.

Time passed. How much time exactly, Rachel didn't know because she didn't have her wristwatch on her arm and she hadn't bothered as of yet with placing a clock in the kids' room. Right now, and for the umpteenth time, she was on her hands and knees looking under the boys' bunk beds for any sign of the missing snake.

"Hi, there. Need any help?"

The voice, coupled with Rachel's own deep concentration in that moment, startled her, and as a result her heart and stomach made a remarkable highjump toward the ceiling while the rest of her body stayed glued to the floor. A moment later, she whirled around, clutching the front of her robe with one hand and rubbing the carpet burns on her knees with the other. "Ross, you scared the living daylights out of me. Don't you know better than to sneak up behind someone like that?"

He laughed, and Rachel couldn't help noticing the tiny lines at the corners of his eyes. But then his dark penetrating gaze began a lazy glide down the entire length of her body and Rachel was suddenly made aware of something else. She was still in her robe—her very short robe.

Of course, it was as much if not more than she'd been wearing on the night she'd tiptoed down the hall and gone to meet him in the spare bedroom.

Finally, his dark, roving eyes made it back up to their starting point. "I didn't sneak up on you," he drawled, exhibiting a bemused expression. "I called out your name several times. You didn't answer."

"I didn't hear you," she said, trying to relax in the hopes that her pounding heart would do the same. She felt as though she had just run a marathon. What compounded the problem, however, was that Ross was here, in the flesh, standing in front of her like it was nothing out of the ordinary for him to be in her house at this time of day. For heaven's sake, her defenses against him weren't even awake yet.

"I'm sorry," he said, grinning at her. "I didn't mean to frighten you."

In spite of her intentions to the contrary, Rachel found herself noticing every detail about him. Something inside turned over when she noticed that his dark brown shirt was the same rich shade of chocolate as his eyes. He wore brown loafers, a leather belt and a pair of blue jeans that hung low on his hips. Finally, after releasing a long-winded breath, she said, "Never mind. It's not your fault. I guess I'm pretty jumpy at this moment."

"So what's the problem?"

You.

But, of course, no way was she going to say that to him. Instead she said, "What are you doing here?"

Ross grinned in a way that somehow told her that he was thoroughly enjoying this moment. "Moving in."

Rachel came up straight. "Moving in? What do you mean?"

His grin widened a degree. "Oh, that's right, you don't know about it, yet, do you?"

Rachel's heart was pounding now. "Know about what, for heaven's sake?"

"That I leased a house just down the street from you. I'm now officially the newest citizen of Abbeville."

Rachel frowned. "You're joking, again."

"Nope. Not this time. Look, I told you that I'd be back. Actually, I've decided to take the unresolved matter of you and me into my own hands."

Rachel gaped at him. "You've undoubtedly lost your mind, Ross Murdock."

He laughed. "I had a feeling you'd say that."

"But what about your career?"

"That's not a problem. With the technology of today, I can easily handle it from here. Besides, I've already hired two young rookies in the Houston office to take over a great deal of my workload. In about six months, I plan to be semi-retired. Besides, I now have much more important matters to see about. Namely, you and the kids."

"That's pretty presumptuous of you—considering we're separated. Not to mention just a fraction too late as far as I'm concerned."

He laughed again. "Well, I don't happen to agree with you on that point, Rachel."

Then, suddenly, his eyes dropped to the floor and he paled. "Don't move," he said in a grave tone of voice that immediately—without question—froze her to the spot.

"What's wrong?" Rachel finally managed to ask.

"Just don't move," he groused.

"Okay, I won't," she replied hastily. "But, what's wrong?"

He was shaking his head in disbelief. "Okay, Rachel, now listen up. There's a live snake on the carpet right behind you and—"

Rachel felt the air go out of her lungs. She knew the snake was Jorgie's. She knew it was small. She even knew it wasn't poisonous. In fact, she had been looking for the darn little thing for well over an hour now. But Ross had said *it was alive* and that thought alone was enough to jar loose some dormant nervous reaction in her that she had known all along lurked somewhere deep inside where snakes were concerned. Lunging forward, she landed right smack-dab in Ross's arms, and together, they went toppling over onto Jorgie's bed.

"What the hell?" Ross said, banging the side of his head against the wall. "Ouch!"

Dead or alive—poisonous or not, Rachel was determined to scramble every inch of herself onto the narrow bunk bed and away from that miserable little snake, in spite of the fact that that was virtually impossible considering that she and Ross were lying sideways across the twin mattress. In the process, her elbow poked Ross in the stomach, then in the chest, punching out a good portion of his air supply. After catching his breath, he wrapped his arms around her, and said, "Rachel, will you hold still a second before you knock one of us out cold?"

Suddenly, as though the wire connecting her nervous reaction had been severed, Rachel halted her frantic movements and stared at Ross. "I'm sorry. I don't know what got into me."

"It's a king snake," he said. "Where'd it come from?"

"It's Jorgie's. He lost it in the house this morning and I've been trying desperately ever since to find it."

Lying almost under Rachel, Ross glanced beyond her shoulder in the direction he'd last seen the reptile. "Right now it's crawling into your hallway. Want me to catch it for you?"

"You know me better than that. Of course, you can catch it for me," she muttered.

He laughed. "Then, stay put," he said, setting her to the side and then rising from the bunk. Then, picking up the empty shoe box on the floor at his feet, he disappeared into the hallway.

Rachel stayed on the bunk as he'd instructed and waited anxiously for his return. After all, she was usually a very obedient person. Her father's rigid rules for his wife and daughters had seen to that.

Several long, drawn-out moments ticked by. Finally she heard Ross come inside and go into the bathroom to wash his hands.

A second later he was standing in the doorway, lazily leaning one shoulder against the frame. "Well," he said, "I captured the snake for you. Now you owe me one." Rachel lifted her eyes and knew instinctively that she'd made a big mistake in *staying put* like he'd said. She sat up immediately and swung her feet to the floor.

But deep inside she knew it was already too late. And before she could rise, Ross was standing right in front of her and she found her face level with the zipper of his jeans.

"What do you think you're doing?" she asked, gazing up at him.

"I don't know, exactly, but then again, I'm not going to stop long enough to figure it out, either," he replied, gently brushing a strand of her hair from her face.

Rachel's breath locked in her throat and it was in that moment that she saw the hunger in his eyes and knew exactly what he was planning to do. A second later a hunger flickered to life in her abdomen and she suddenly needed him as much as ever. Dropping down on one knee in front of her, Ross cupped her face with his hands. Instinctively knowing what he was planning to do next, she closed her eyes and waited for his warm lips to touch hers.

Ross kissed her, leisurely at first. Then he began to push his tongue into her mouth and she let him, in spite of her inner warnings. She knew the danger there was in allowing herself to be so reckless in his arms.

His tongue was hot and moist and relentless in its pursuit, and it danced and tasted and played a frenzied game of tease and surrender with her until she felt like she would go mad with wanting him. His arm encircled her waist, and, when he pulled her off the bunk bed, she fell against him easily. Rachel pressed her body to his with a burning need to be joined with him. And yet, somewhere in the back of her mind, she knew that this moment was completely out of context with reality and at some point this craziness would surely have to end.

Ross's hands were everywhere, but mostly they cupped her bare buttocks beneath the robe and held her enticingly against him. Rachel thought she might just die from the sheer pleasure of having his hands on her body. But then, as though shocked by his own lack of control, he suddenly released her, stood, and dragged in a ragged breath.

Stunned by her own behavior—or rather, *mis*behavior—it took Rachel a moment to gather her wits. But even during those chaotic moments when she wasn't sure of what to do with herself, she had come to one conclusion. She had to salvage her pride. She simply had to. Keeping that uppermost in her mind, she took a deep breath and said, "This has got to stop, Ross, once and for all."

Glancing in her direction, Ross's gaze dropped to her chest, and he gallantly closed her robe, which was exposing her naked breasts. Then his eyes lifted to Rachel's face and he smiled. "Well, if it were up to me," he said, "we'd just finish what we've started."

"No way," Rachel stated firmly.

"Why not?" he argued. "If we don't, it's just going to eat at us. I say we finish it—now."

Rachel knew that Ross was right about the tension in her gut eating at her, because it was already taking a few bites. But, in truth, she could probably handle holes in her stomach a lot easier than she could her conscience.

Still, Rachel hesitated with her answer. Undoubtedly, it gave Ross the advantage he'd been looking for and he jumped on it like an alley cat on a defenseless little church mouse.

"Where are the kids?" he asked huskily, moving in on her.

"Uh . . . with Jan."

He'd already slipped off his loafers and socks and as he began to unbuckle his belt, Rachel felt a weakness in her stomach. "For how long?"

"For the day," she replied breathlessly.

"Good," he said. "Then we've got plenty of time for what I have in mind."

Her heart was pounding in her throat as she watched him shrug out of his shirt and toss it to the floor.

Reaching for her hands, Ross brought her to her feet and began to tug at her robe. "I want to see you naked," he drawled heavily.

Somewhere in the back of her mind, Rachel still had one ounce of rational thinking left. "Wait—Ross," she said fleetingly. "You can't really be serious about this."

His gaze was intense... grave... hot... naked with desire. "Oh, but I am," he growled. "I've missed you so much, Rachel."

Then his mouth took hers in an all-consuming kiss and Rachel felt her meager control slip to the floor like a feather. The very next thing she knew, Ross's big, wide hands were on her shoulders and her white silk robe joined the growing pile on the carpet. She moaned in sweet anticipation of what she knew awaited her in the coming minutes.

Lifting Rachel into his strong arms, Ross's hungry mouth never left hers and he turned and headed down the hall to her bedroom. He laid her across her mattress, removed his jeans and boxers and straddled her.

"I want you, Rachel, more than anything in the world. But I want to hear you say that you want me, too."

Want him? She would've gladly died to have him in that moment. "Oh, I do, Ross. I want you so much—"

Suddenly they heard the roar of an engine as a vehicle pulled into Rachel's driveway and braked to a stop right under her bedroom window. They halted their movements and their eyes met.

A car door slammed. And then another.

The sound of voices rose above the noise of the outdoor air-conditioning compressor that hummed nearby.

"Someone's here," Rachel said, barely breathing. But for the life of her, she couldn't make the necessary move to see who it was.

Finally, Ross, seeming to regain his equilibrium, leaned forward and peeked out the nearby window. "Oh, boy," he said in a none-too-jovial tone of voice. "It's Jan and the kids."

A couple of seconds ticked by before Rachel was finally able to move. When she did, she reacted as though she'd suddenly been thrown back to earth from some outer dimension. "Oh, God... Get dressed, Ross, and hurry. We can't let them catch us like this," she exclaimed, jumping to her feet. Jerking open her bedroom door, she raced down the hall to get the silk robe left on the floor in her sons' room. She quickly gathered up Ross's shirt.

"Don't panic, Rachel. We're still married, remember?" Ross called in her wake.

"But we're separated," she quickly replied from over her shoulder.

"So what?" he asked, now coming up the hall without a stitch of clothing on. She immediately shoved his shirt at him. "Get dressed," she commanded again, picking up his shoes and socks and doing the same with them.

He gave her a salute. "Yes, ma'am."

Rachel slipped on her robe and tied the sash around her waist. The whole time, Ross just stood there, watching her with a certain, mischievous twinkle in his eyes.

"Ross, please... Don't be immature about this, okay?"

"Immature? Who's being immature? You know something, Rachel, you really need to lighten up," he replied with a wide, playful grin. "Oh, and by the way, did you know that your boobs jiggle like crazy when you run around naked like you were doing just a moment ago?"

"Now that's being immature."

"No, it's not. It's being human. I couldn't help but notice, honey."

Honey, my rear end, she told herself, rolling her eyes upward. Quickly turning away from his gloating expression, she headed for the kitchen. She reached it just as Jan came through the back door.

"Hi," her sister said, immediately pointing back over her shoulder at Jorgie and Danny who had stayed outside. "Look," she continued, visibly shaking off her disgust for the reptile the boys seemed to like so much. "I'm sorry to barge in like this so soon after leaving with the kids, but they were worrying me silly over that miserable little snake. They just had to come here to see for themselves if you'd found it." Then, taking in Rachel's appearance, she paused open-mouthed and said, "Uh, looks to me like you had a pretty good struggle trying to get the thing back into its box."

Ross chose that moment to step through the doorway. "Hello, Jan."

Jan stared at him blankly. "Well, hello. Uh, I didn't know that you were coming to see the boys today."

Ross grinned. "Well, there's a bit more to my being here than that."

"Oh?" she replied.

"Ross has decided to move to Abbeville," Rachel quickly informed her sister.

Jan's eyes widened. "Is that so?"

"My furniture should be arriving today, as a matter of fact," Ross stated calmly. "I'm moving in just down the street."

"That's great!" Jan said.

"I'm glad someone thinks so."

Jan glanced at Rachel. "The boys are going to love having you here. I know they miss you."

"I'm sure they will," Rachel said in a way that was meant to put an ending to the conversation.

Jan looked from one to the other. "Ah, look, did I interrupt something?"

"Why, no—"

"Yes," Ross replied, stepping up to the back door and looking out to see his sons. Then he turned back to glance at Jan from over his shoulder. "But don't worry about it." He slipped out the back door.

"I won't, then," Jan replied absently.

And then she turned to her sister. "Rachel, for heaven's sake, what are you doing? You're playing with fire."

Without bothering to answer her sister, Rachel stepped up to the window and observed Ross as he spoke to their children.

Jan cleared her throat. "Look, may I make a suggestion?" she asked.

Turning back in her direction, Rachel nodded. "Go ahead."

"Well," Jan said, "this is probably none of my business, but since you keep telling me that you're planning to divorce Ross, I think I should remind you that you need to be careful."

"Careful?" Rachel asked. "Careful of what?"

"Of getting pregnant, that's what."

Jan's remark cut Rachel to the bone as sure as a machete would have. It was the one topic she'd been trying so desperately not to think about since her night of reckless passion in Ross's arms.

Rachel forced a smile. "Thank you, Jan, for being concerned. But I can assure you, there's nothing to worry about."

Jan gave an unconvincing sigh. "Yeah…well, from the looks of things, I hope my warning hasn't already come too late."

Without commenting—she simply couldn't at this point without adding one white lie on top of another—Rachel turned back to watch her children interact with their father. Getting pregnant at a time like this was an added complication she certainly didn't need.

Still, regardless of that fact, Rachel immediately realized that telling her heart as much was going to be an impossible task. Just the thought of her carrying Ross's child again was actually making her feel all warm and fuzzy inside.

But, of course, undoubtedly, if it turned out that she wasn't pregnant, that would be for the absolute best.

Right? Rachel asked herself as a kind of reassurance.

Uh, yeah. Sure. Whatever you say, her inner voice finally answered.

Chapter Six

Eventually, Rachel went outside on the patio to join the others. Much to her relief—and Jan's, as well—Ross was able to convince Jorgie into letting the king snake go free, after telling the child that the reptile longed to be released back into its own natural habitat. Then he turned his intense gaze in Rachel's direction. "I have a favor to ask of you."

Stepping out from beneath her patio cover into the bright midmorning sunlight, Rachel shaded her eyes. "Oh?" she said, giving him a curious look.

"I was hoping," he said, "that I could pick the boys up this afternoon and take them over to my house. I figure the sooner I get them there to see the place the sooner they'll realize that I'm back in their lives on a constant basis."

Rachel shrugged. "You're so insistent about doing this, do I really have a choice in the matter?"

"I was hoping that you'd come, too," Ross responded.

"I'm busy," Rachel replied.

He propped his hands on his lean hips. "You're not that busy, for heaven's sake. You could make time if you wanted," he replied. "You're just being stubborn about this."

"That isn't a fair remark, Ross."

He stepped back, pretending to be shocked. "Hey, I didn't know that we were playing fair. In fact, who said that we had to play this game by your rules in the first place?"

"Well, I certainly don't have to take orders from you."

"I didn't give you an order," he said. "I did, however, invite you to come with me and the kids tonight and have a little fun."

"In that case, I can't."

"Actually, what you really mean is, you *won't* come. Am I right?"

Rachel took a deep breath. "Look, Ross, I don't know what you're expecting of me. But it's obviously not the same thing I'm willing to give you."

"Well, actually, Rachel," he said, placing his hands on his hips, "I'm learning not to expect much from you."

"Now, that's a cheap shot."

"You've earned it."

"And you haven't?"

"I probably have—in the past. But this is today. How much longer are you going to punish me for the sins of my past?"

Rachel gaped at him. "I'm not punishing you."

"Well, you damned sure could've fooled me. And the kids, too."

"Don't bring the kids into this," Rachel warned.

"What?" Ross said sarcastically. "Are you blind? Or have you simply refused to notice that they are right, smack-dab in the middle of all this?"

Rachel glanced toward her children who were concentrating at the moment on the spot where Jorgie had just released the small king snake near an azalea bush. "Look, Ross, I don't happen to like the way you've just moved yourself into our lives now that you feel like it and expect us to just fall all over ourselves because of it."

"I don't expect you to just fall all over yourself because of me. But I do expect you to give me, this family, a fair shot at being happy together. And that's what you're not doing."

"I am being fair." She told herself to take a deep breath and calm down, so that's what she tried to do. But she failed miserably.

"Oh, yeah? Then prove it," he said. "Put that enormous pride of yours aside for one night and come along with us."

"My pride?"

He sighed deeply. "Yeah. Your pride, Rachel. Look, can't you see? We're after the same things in life now. So what are you so afraid of?"

"I'm not afraid of anything."

"Then come with us."

Rachel lifted her chin to a haughty level. "If I do, it will only be because of the kids—and not anything else."

"Fine with me."

Rachel turned and used her hand to shield her eyes from the sun. "I'll think about it."

He smiled. "You do that," he replied, turning on his heels and walking back to where the boys were. Halfway across the yard, he stopped and turned to look at her. "I'm not going to just go away, Rachel. Not this time. So you should just get used to the idea of having me around."

Rachel glared at him. Ross was the most arrogant, the most self-assured, the most irritating, man that Rachel had ever known. The audacity of him to think that she was going to sit by and allow him to intimidate her like that. Just who had appointed him the King Kong of her life, anyway?

She marched herself back under the patio cover and flounced down into a chair. Jan looked up from the magazine she was browsing through. "I tell you, Rachel, Ross is so intense he takes my breath away—and I'm not even in love with him like you are."

Once again, Rachel glared in his direction. "I'm not in love with him like that. Not anymore."

"Come on, Rachel. Just who are you trying to fool? Me, or yourself?"

"Look," Rachel said, sighing deeply, "I don't need to hear this from you, okay?"

"He isn't going to just disappear, you know."

"I know. Not anytime soon, anyway."

"Well, in the meantime, what are you going to do about him? Dig a hole and stick your head in the ground?"

"Very funny," Rachel replied, narrowing her eyes while she continued to watch Ross from a distance. Jan was right. He was so . . . so intense.

Rachel shook her head. "I'm going to go along with him for the time being. He wants to spend time with me and the kids? Fine. We'll spend time with him. But, I know Ross. Sooner or later, this whole thing is going to get old for him."

Jan looked up again from her magazine and glanced at Ross. "Mmm, I don't know, Rachel. Look, maybe this time you're wrong about him. Maybe he really means what he's saying."

"I don't believe that for a second. And I really don't want to talk about him anymore. So let's drop the subject, okay?"

Jan flipped through a couple more pages in the magazine. "Fine with me."

Rachel looked on as Ross bent down and spoke to his sons. Then he turned and started in her direction. He didn't stop until he reached her. "Look, I'm going now, Rachel. My furniture should be arriving soon at my house, and I've got to be there."

"Okay," she replied.

"But I'll be back at five o'clock for the kids."

She had little doubt about that. "I'll have them ready."

He turned toward Jan. "See you later, Jan."

She lifted her head. "Yeah, sure, Ross. See you soon."

"Goodbye, Rachel," he drawled, deliberately stopping and waiting to hear her answer. When it didn't come right away, he narrowed his eyes.

If looks could kill, then the one he gave Rachel would've done her in.

"Goodbye, Ross," she finally said.

The instant he disappeared from their view, Jan sighed in relief. "For God's sake, Rachel, but that man is so intense. How can you refuse him anything?''

Sometimes—like now—when she wanted him so badly that she could taste it—Rachel didn't have the slightest idea how she ever found the courage to deny him anything.

Jan and the boys left for the park and Rachel got busy doing chores around her house. A bit later in the morning she found herself feeling sick to her stomach and ended up curling up on her bed for almost an hour before the feeling finally left her and she felt normal again. And, of course, at some point while she'd lain there, Jan's warning about getting pregnant came back to haunt her. She assured herself that she was jumping to all kinds of unnecessary conclusions. The likelihood of her being pregnant with Ross's child was remote. They'd only been intimate once, for heaven's sake. True, her period was late. But it had been late before. Once she'd even skipped a whole month for no reason at all when she was still in high school. There was no cause for alarm. Not yet, anyway.

Finally, she showered and dressed. Afterward she did a few more chores and then eventually drove herself down to the neighborhood drugstore with a list of the supplies she would be needing in the upcoming week.

Checking off her supply list as she went down each aisle, Rachel never intended to end up in the section of the store where she presently stood. But, since she had wandered there, it was pointless for her to walk away as if she were trying to avoid the area. She scanned the neatly supplied rows of boxes and bottles, creams and lotions, until her eye caught sight of an item on the very top shelf. She reached for the box, flipped it around so that she could see the labeling on the back and began to read.

Several uninterrupted moments went by. Then, suddenly, from somewhere behind her, Rachel heard her name being called and it startled her badly. She immediately replaced the box on the shelf, whirled around and found Orlan's mother, Mindy, standing just behind her.

"Oh, hello, Mindy," she said, feeling a blush stain her cheeks. In truth, Rachel was embarrassed for being caught red-handed while reading the labeling on the back of a box that was so obviously, conspicuously, manufactured for one purpose only. For women only. She and Mindy chitchatted for a moment and then Mindy wandered off.

Pausing momentarily, Rachel reached once again for the box, but instead of reading the label on the back, she dropped it into her shopping cart with her other items and headed for the front checkout register. She hadn't any idea why she felt so uncomfortable in buying herself a pregnancy test. The girl at the cash register knew her only by name.

Well, anyway, all that was beside the point. She was probably buying the darn thing for nothing anyway. She probably wouldn't need it.

In fact, after arriving at home with her purchases, Rachel was so good at convincing herself of that fact that she went straight to her bathroom closet and placed the unopened box on the top shelf behind several other personal items already stored there. Then, closing the closet door, she leaned against it and took a deep breath. "There," she said out loud. "That'll probably be the last time I'll ever have to think about it."

Rachel kept herself busy. She'd always had help in her house and since moving to Abbeville a maid service came to her home twice a week to help with her housework. But there were certain chores around the house that she had always done for herself.

Around three o'clock, Jan dropped the boys off after their day at the park. Rachel made them get cleaned up for when their father would come for them. Finally, dressed and ready to go, she settled them in the den with a video game until he arrived. Eventually, she sleepily sat down with them.

The next thing Rachel knew, Jorgie was shaking her awake. "Mommy, Mommy, wake up. Daddy's here."

Rachel opened her eyes. "Uh? What?"

Jorgie and Danny were standing right next to her. "Daddy's here," he repeated.

"Hi," Ross said, stepping up behind Jorgie and gazing down at her. He wore a pair of blue jeans and a sport shirt that was just the right shade of blue to enhance his dark, good looks. At the sight of him, Rachel's stomach took an immediate nosedive to the floor.

Narrowing his gaze, Ross studied her face. "Look, I'm sorry to disturb you, but I decided that it was best if we woke you up. I'm afraid we'll end up missing the next feature at the theater if we don't get going soon."

Sitting up straight, Rachel rubbed her eyes. "That's okay," she said, glancing at her wristwatch and making the surprise discovery that she had been asleep for well over an hour.

Ross sat next to her on the sofa. "Rachel, are you feeling all right?"

Rachel could smell the subtle fragrance of his spicy, masculine cologne, and, without another thought, shot straight up from her seat. "Of course I am."

Ross rose slowly to his full height. "Okay," he said, sounding somewhat unconvinced. He tucked his hands into the back pockets of his jeans and Rachel's eyes followed his every movement. "I'll accept that answer for now. So, are you coming with us?" he asked.

Rachel frowned. Ross was being so pushy these days that she was barely able to keep up with one thing and he was already shoving her toward another. It was tiring, to say the least. And irritating, too. Every time she turned around he was practically in her face, giving her orders. Or, at least, trying to. He was pushing her, always pushing her, to play by his rules. But she didn't trust him enough anymore to play his game. She had once, and look where it had gotten her.

Rachel shook her head. "No. I'm not going."

He smirked as if he had known that was going to be her answer all along. Then he turned and said to their sons, "Hey, guys, how would you like it if your mama came with us tonight?"

Rachel gaped at him.

Honestly, she couldn't believe he would stoop so low as to use their sons to make her bend to his will.

He lifted his eyes and gave her a cocky, satisfied smile. One that told her he was willing to play as dirty as necessary to get what he wanted from her. And if she'd had any doubts about how far he would actually go, she didn't anymore.

"Will you, Mommy?" Danny asked hopefully.

"Please, Mommy," Jorgie added.

Rachel looked down at their expectant little faces and then she glanced up at the arrogance in Ross's. "You aren't playing fair—and you know it."

He grinned. "According to my rules, it's every man for himself. So get used to it, Rachel. You're not going to have a free ride out of our marriage. Not if I can help it."

She scanned his features and knew by his lofty expression that he meant every word of that. Inhaling deeply, Rachel glanced down at her sons. "Well," she said, forcing a smile that she didn't quite feel—but then, how could she, when she felt that she had just lost another major battle to the enemy? "Let's go get pizza."

The children hurried toward the door. When Rachel remained standing where she was, Jorgie came back and took her by the hand. "Come on, Mommy. It'll be fun, you'll see."

Rachel's heart was breaking into a thousand pieces. Her children hadn't done anything wrong and they deserved better from their parents than what they were getting. But then, that's why she'd left Ross in the first place. She had been seeking better for them. Was she failing them now, as well?

Rachel looked down at the old pair of white shorts and the white tank top she was wearing. "Look," she said, "I'm going to have to change clothes if I'm going to go with you."

Ross shrugged. "You look fine to me."

"I'm not going like this," she insisted.

He motioned down the hall toward her bedroom. "Fine. Go change clothes, then. But hurry up. We'll be late."

"I'll be right back," she said, scooting off.

Shutting the door to her bedroom, she took a deep breath and rushed toward her closet. She pulled a pair of blue jeans from a hanger and then hurried into her bathroom.

Jerking off her white tank top, she threw it into a laundry basket bound for the wash. Then she began to pull down on the zipper at the front of her white shorts and, in her haste, got it stuck on the white lace trim that ran down the front of her bikini panties. It didn't take her long to realize that she couldn't get the zipper to budge either way, up or down, no matter how much she tried. Stuck, to say the least, she was trying to figure out her next move when she heard a knock at her bedroom door. "I'm coming," she yelled. "Just give me a minute. My zipper's stuck."

She heard the bedroom door open. "Can I help?" Ross asked.

"No, I can get it," she shouted back to him. The last thing she needed was Ross's hands touching her in any fashion. She was already so keyed up right then, she just might explode.

His tall, masculine frame suddenly filled the doorway of her bathroom.

Standing there, half undressed, in only her bra and panties—and, of course, in the pair of white shorts with the zipper that wouldn't budge—Rachel glance up at him.

"Got a problem?" he said, leaning against the side of the doorjamb, his arms crossed over his chest.

"Well... Don't just stand there," she said accusingly. "Help me, for heaven's sake."

One corner of his sexy mouth lifted in a grin. "My pleasure, ma'am," he drawled. He stepped inside the bathroom and then dropped down until his face was almost level with her waistline. "Hmm..." he said, "let's see here." He tugged at the zipper a couple of times. When it didn't budge, he looked up at her, and that automatically brought his face—his mouth—enticingly close to her breasts. Too close, in fact, if she was going to be able to remain in control.

His tongue snaked out and licked the skin on her belly. "Mmm...salty," he said, smacking his lips together. "Tasty, though."

And that was it for Rachel. Her willpower began to slowly unravel, stitch by stitch. Inch by inch.

It took about six seconds for her to fall completely apart at the seams. When she did, she tangled her fingers in his hair for support. "Damn you, Ross," she cried. Her face lowered to meet his.

Ross groaned and pulled her against him roughly. After assaulting her mouth for several hot, frenzied moments, he buried his face in her cleavage and groaned again. "Damn you, too, Rachel," he said.

He took her lips again in a scorching kiss.

And then, suddenly, perhaps from out of her own desperate attempt to regain her sanity, Rachel had a rational thought. One that was powerful enough to make her halt her actions. "Ross, wait—stop—the kids."

His movements stopped instantly, and his head snapped up. "Yeah, right," he said, drawing in a deep breath. "I almost forgot. The kids."

He released her immediately and she stood on her own in spite of her shaky knees. Rising, Ross took a step back and ran his fingers through his hair.

"This has got to stop, Ross," Rachel insisted.

"Yeah, well...don't get your zipper caught next time."

"It's not just this time that I'm talking about. It's every time. It's us. We're out of control. We're separated, for heaven's sake. And from now on, we need to behave like we are."

"You behave like we are. I don't think my libido is going to listen to that kind of reasoning."

"It's not going to have any choice," Rachel said. "I'm not going to let anything like this happen again. Now, if you don't mind, you can leave and I'll get dressed."

He motioned toward her body. "Well, do you want me to get your zipper loose, or what?" he asked.

"If you think that you can do it without... without—"

"Yeah," he said, grabbing hold of the zipper tab, "I think I can do it without that."

"Okay, then," she said breathlessly, certain now that he would behave himself. And, of course, she would have never misbehaved in the first place if he hadn't come into her dressing room. This was his fault. All of it.

Ross yanked hard on the zipper and somehow it got free. "There," he said, "you can take your shorts off now."

Rachel's eyes shot up. "I will, as soon as you leave my bathroom."

He rolled his eyes. "For heaven's sake, Rachel, why don't you stop acting like we're total strangers to each other. We started dating each other so young, we practically grew up naked together."

Rachel gave him a chastising frown. "For Pete's sake, Ross, will you watch what you say? The kids might hear you and think that we...we did it before we got married."

"I'll tell them better when they're old enough."

"Oh," Rachel said, putting a towel around her for the time being. "I guess that's supposed to make me feel a whole lot better now."

"Hey, it's better if they hear the facts of life from us than from some street punk."

"I know that," she snapped back, and then she wondered how their conversation had changed directions so quickly.

She deepened her frown. "Look, the sooner you leave and let me get dressed, the sooner we'll be on our way. You said for me to hurry up. Well, I'm trying."

He smiled when she reminded him of what he'd said. But then a second later he turned around and walked out.

Rachel finally joined them, and they hurried out the door and piled into Ross's car. He drove them to see his new house, which was part of the plan for tonight. Rachel was amazed to discover that he'd furnished it in tastes similar to her own. He showed Jorgie and Danny the bedroom he called *theirs* and promised them that they could now spend the night with him as often as they liked. But the entire time that they explored one room after another, Rachel had this nagging question in the back of her mind.

Finally, when the boys went outside and they were alone together in his kitchen, she leaned her hips against the cabinet and gazed at him from across the room. "Ross, let me ask you something. What's going to happen to the kids when you get tired of all of this, pull up stakes and return to Houston? Those two kids out there aren't going to understand when you become a once-a-month weekend father, again. Hasn't it ever crossed your mind that you're going to hurt them even more by pretending that this is what they can expect from you from now on, when it really isn't?''

Ross shook his head in disbelief. "You still don't get it, do you, Rachel? I'm not going to get tired of this game. Nor am I going to pull up stakes. I'm back in my sons' lives for good now. And I'm back in yours, too. You simply refuse to see it. But, you will—soon.''

Rachel crossed her arms under her breasts. "That sounds like pure arrogance to me.''

He grinned. "It probably is.''

His good mood was beginning to irritate her. "What's the matter with you?'' Rachel asked. "Can't you stop grinning at me long enough to finish this argument like you're supposed to?''

His grin widened. "I don't think so.''

"Oh-hh . . .'' Rachel said in frustration. She turned suddenly and went out the back door to meet her children.

But she knew that turning her back and running away from Ross wasn't going to solve anything. Actually, all it did was let him see her many weaknesses. Every single one of them. She had so many, in fact, that he was probably having a hard time keeping up with them.

Good.

She was glad to know that something about her was still a challenge for him.

A few minutes later he came outside with his car keys dangling in his hand. "Okay, guys,'' he said, "are you ready now for the night on the town that I promised you?''

The boys shouted out their answers like kids usually do when they're happy.

Rachel was thankful, though, that he hadn't asked her if she was ready.

Because the truth of the matter was, in spite of the warning bells that were going off in her head like sirens, she found herself ready for almost anything that he might have had in mind.

In fact, anything at all.

Chapter Seven

The pizza restaurant in nearby Lafayette was busy when they arrived, but they were seated quickly in spite of the crowd. From that point on the night seemed to move along with a kind of unexpected magic, and not even the crowded restaurant, nor the humid hot air that prevailed outside seemed to have an effect on them. An hour later, they left Scaleni's and climbed into Ross's car for the movie theater. They were just in time for the upcoming feature, and, by the time Ross was next in line to buy their tickets, Rachel was realizing to herself that she couldn't remember the last time she'd had this much fun in a long time. Ross, too, seemed to be having the time of his life. Certainly, he was behaving more like his old self than he had in quite a while. Even their two sons were caught up in the moment and, as a result, now had a combined energy level between them that probably could've launched the space shuttle into orbit. It was truly turning out to be a special night for them, and Rachel realized that her sons had been hungry for this sort of attention from both parents—together—at the same time—all along. Unfortunately, a night like this wasn't something they could expect in the future.

Carrying popcorn, orange sodas and chocolate-mint candy, Ross, Rachel and their kids strolled the well-lit aisle until they found four seats in a row midway down. Danny went in the row first and took a seat. Rachel followed. Ross came next, and Jorgie slipped in last.

When they were all seated, Ross turned his head from one side to the other. "Well, gang, are we having fun yet?" he asked.

"I am," Danny exclaimed, looking up at his mother and grinning at her. Rachel smiled back at him.

"Me, too," Jorgie replied, a second later filling his mouth with popcorn.

Ross glanced at Rachel. "How about you?"

Rachel knew that she could have lied at that point. But the plain, simple truth was, she didn't want to. Somehow this night was endearing itself to her and she couldn't bear the thought of tarnishing it with lies. Not even her own. Not even to protect her vulnerability.

She looked up and smiled. "You were right," she said to him. "I'm having a wonderful time."

His eyes warmed to the color of dark chocolate. Dark, scrumptious chocolate. The kind she had yearned to buy for herself at the concession stand only moments ago. But she had known she hadn't needed the extra calories, any more than she needed the extra feelings his gaze was now producing in her. "I'm glad," he replied. "Because I'm having a good time, too."

Her flesh tingled. Obviously the magic of this night was beginning to rub off on her. She smiled openly at him.

Suddenly the lights in the theater dimmed and the feature presentation flashed up on the screen in front of them.

Rachel leaned in close to Ross's ear. "What's the movie about?" she whispered. She crunched down on a kernel of hot, buttered popcorn.

"Shush," the lady behind her replied with a loud hissing sound that made several people in the rows ahead of them wonder what was going on and look back at Rachel for the answer.

Rachel blushed a deep red. She had never been one who enjoyed being on center stage—she wasn't the extrovert her husband was—but especially when she suddenly found herself there and those glaring at her weren't smiling. Under those circumstances she always felt about wee small.

Like now.

"Sorry," she shot back over her shoulder to the woman behind her. Then she sat up straight so that the woman would know that she had no intentions of interrupting her concentration again. As it was, Rachel was certain that the reason Ross was chuckling under his breath was because of her obvious embarrassment.

After the first few scenes into the movie, Rachel knew that it was going to be an adventure story. Classic in its plot, it was the tale of the strained relationship between an obsessive man, his distraught wife and their three spoiled children who become stranded in a desolate cabin during a winter snowstorm. Rachel knew that as the story progressed the members of that family were going to have to learn to depend on and help one another to survive. Caught up in the drama, Rachel didn't realize that she had begun to press the side of her leg against Ross's until she unconsciously went to move it and Ross stopped her by placing his hand on her knee—at which point she almost jumped out of her skin.

Rachel was too shaken by what Ross had done to her to even look at him. Her stomach knotted as she waited for him to remove his hand from her knee. When he didn't, she grew even more anxious for him to do so. Ross knew, of course, that the movie patrol was sitting right behind her and that she was hesitant to make even the slightest sound. Damn him, anyway, for taking full advantage of a situation that was making her feel so uncomfortable. It was just like him to do something like that. True, there was a small wicked part of her that was actually enjoying his little teasing game. But that's all it was to him. A game. Now it was time to end it. But his hand stayed where it was, and her stomach stayed in knots.

A minute or so passed, and then Ross began to slowly glide his fingers up and down her inner thigh. So slow, in fact, it was as though he had a lazy-dazy purpose in mind for tracing the inner seam of her blue jeans all the way up to the . . . the—oh, good grief—to the most private area of her body, for heaven's sake! Obviously, he did have a purpose. He wanted to drive her plum crazy. And he was.

Rachel held her breath as shock waves of delight shimmied through every single cell in her body. And just when she thought she couldn't take another moment of his masterful teasing, his fingers began a downward journey to their originating point, which allowed her to breathe again with so much less effort.

He leaned in close to her. "Am I bothering you?"

She glared at him hard through the darkness of the movie theater. In truth, she didn't think she could take much more of his fingers gliding—or sliding—over her body in any direction without coming completely apart at the inner seams. "Yes," she whispered. "Now, stop it, Ross, this instant."

The woman behind her leaned forward. "Lady, my son-in-law is the manager of this theater and I'm going to report you to him if you make one more sound."

Rachel threw the woman a lethal glare from over her shoulder. By golly, she'd had enough. Of the both of them. "Then do it," she said.

The woman's eyes widened to the size of silver dollars, and she sat back in her seat in a huffed-up manner. "Well, I never..." she said under her breath.

Rachel turned aggravated eyes back to Ross, and he immediately held his hands up in front of him.

"Okay. I quit. I promise," he said laughingly.

Inhaling deeply, Rachel turned back to face the screen with the intention of watching the movie. And if Ross tried one more ridiculous thing on her, she was going to dump the rest of her popcorn over his head. As it was, she had thought of doing so earlier. But then, it would've made such a mess and caused such a commotion. Undoubtedly the theater manager would have been summoned at that point and she would've been the one thrown out of the theater for causing an unnecessary disturbance. She wasn't about to give the snooty woman behind her that much satisfaction. Or Ross, either, for that matter. Besides, it would only ruin the entire night and upset her kids who seemed to be having such a good time.

Finally, the feature ended. By this time Danny had fallen asleep, so Ross lifted him in his arms.

The rest of the moviegoers were now anxious for an escape route and poured up the aisle past them in a rush to be on their way. Finally, the crowd thinned and the Murdock family was able to leave.

Ross drove them home and carried Danny inside the house. Jorgie got into his pajamas while Rachel and Ross struggled together to get Danny into his. Finally, both boys were tucked into their beds and kissed good-night. Then Rachel turned off their bedroom light and closed the door.

Rachel realized that she and Ross were alone. Anxious to have him on his way without delay, she wiped her hands down the sides of her jeans and smiled anxiously at him. "Uh . . . Thank you, for tonight, Ross. The boys loved it—and I must say, I had a good time, too."

He grinned. "I knew you would. When can we do it again?"

"Ross, you know how I feel about this."

"No. Tell me. How do you feel?"

"We can't continue to go out together like we're a normal family. We're only going to confuse the boys. And all for nothing."

Ross gaped at her. "Rachel, haven't you listened to anything I've been saying? This is it. I'm here to stay. And regardless of what you say, I'm not backing off. I've already given you six months to get your head screwed back on straight. Now I'm through waiting. From now on, I'm going to help you get it done."

"I don't need your help," she snapped.

"Yes, you do."

"I don't."

Rachel's heart was pounding.

Ross smiled.

"What's so damned funny?" she asked.

"You and your temper. You let it get the best of you sometimes."

He was right, and Rachel knew it. But sometimes her temper was her only guard. Her only means of protecting herself from additional hurt. Maybe it wasn't exactly Freud's way of survival, but often times it was hers.

Ross ran his fingers through his hair. "Come on, Rachel, lighten up," he said a moment later. "Life isn't always as rough as it seems. Besides," he added with a sheepish grin, "I have another favor to ask of you."

Rachel shook her head. Frustrated with him, with herself—with everything—she didn't want to hear one single word from him. "You know something, Ross, you really have some nerve to want to ask me a favor at a time like this."

He grinned. "I know. But that's the kind of guy I am."

Rachel sighed and then threw her hands in the air. "Okay. What is it you want from me this time?"

"Actually, it's not exactly a favor, it's more of an invitation. See, I want you to attend an auction with me in Houston on Sunday afternoon."

"An auction?" she said, dumbfounded. "Why an auction?"

He cleared his throat. "Well . . . I guess 'cause I happen to know that it's to benefit your favorite charity."

Rachel frowned. She had several charities. But her favorite was probably the one she'd helped found in downtown Houston for battered children. "Kids' Kare Shelter?" she finally replied.

"That's the one," Ross said.

"How do you know about the auction?"

"Because I'm now a member of its board of advisers."

Rachel's eyes widened. "Since when?"

"A couple of months."

Rachel knew that Ross had always donated money to charity, but until now he'd never donated any of his time. And the fact that he'd chosen the one charity that was so close to her heart certainly came as a warm, cozy surprise.

"Will you come?" he asked, his expression open . . . waiting . . . hopeful. . . .

"Well . . . I don't know. The kids—"

"They can come with us. In fact, I've already spoken to Mrs. Jenkins and she's available for baby-sitting this weekend."

Rachel smiled to herself. She should have known that Ross would have every detail already covered. He always did. It was his nature. Sometimes, though, his actions were more the result of pure arrogance. But that, too, was his nature.

He grinned at her. "You aren't upset with me, are you?" he asked.

And that was one of those strange phenomena about Ross. Sometimes even his arrogance could be appealing—if the timing was right and the grin on his face was just so. Like now. And it was always at times like these that Rachel was reminded of the fact that she'd never really had a choice in loving him. It had been her destiny from day one. "No."

She took a deep, decisive breath. "Okay. I'll go with you," she said, conceding to the fact that in some ways she was anxious to go to Houston, even if it was for just a short visit. Until now, she hadn't been able to bring herself to return since she'd packed up the boys and moved to Louisiana. The memories there were still so painfully raw that she had feared the wound in her heart might start bleeding again and never stop.

Ross stepped closer to her and suddenly Rachel realized that he'd cornered her between the side of the sofa and the wall. She glanced up and their eyes met. Then she saw the predatorlike gleam in his. "Why don't you just go ahead and say it, Rachel?" he drawled. She didn't know what he was talking about but her heart was suddenly pounding with anticipation.

"Say, what, for heaven's sake?" she asked.

His hot, penetrating gaze was so intense on her face that it singed the baby-fine hair along her hairline.

"That you want me just like you did on the night Danny was found. Say it, Rachel," he said, tangling his fingers into her hair at the back of her head. "Because even though you try to pretend otherwise, I know that you do."

She gaped at him. "I—I do not."

He backed her up so close to the wall that her buttocks were touching it. "Well, you know what?" he said, narrowing his eyes. "I don't happen to believe you."

"Well, it's true," she said breathlessly. Then she pushed her body against his in an effort to escape. Big mistake on her part. Very big mistake. He was hard—solid. He didn't even budge. "Now let me pass."

"No way," he drawled. "First, you've got to prove to me that you don't want me. And I know just how you can do it."

"How?"

"Let me kiss you."

Rachel laughed self-consciously. "That's an absurd thing to say. Now, let me go, Ross."

He still didn't budge. "Well, see," he said, "the way I got it figured, if it's really true that you don't want me, then you won't respond if I kiss you. Right?"

Rachel frowned momentarily. "Well, I guess not," she finally said warily. She had this funny feeling, though, that she was being set up.

"Then prove it. Let me kiss you good-night. But," he said, pointing his finger to the center of her chest, "in order for you to prove your point, you can't respond. And if you do, then you lose."

Rachel paused once again to consider what he was saying. Finally she shook her head. "No—no, I don't think so, Ross. I don't like it."

"What's there not to like? I kiss you. You don't respond. Two quick steps, and then it's over with. I go home. You go to bed."

Now that sounded simply too easy, Rachel thought. She *was* being set up. "I don't think so, Ross. I'd rather if we just said good-night now."

"Come on, Rachel. What's the matter? Are you chicken?"

Well . . . yes, she thought. And possibly just a little crazy as well for even standing here and having this ludicrous conversation with him.

And maybe, just maybe, she was just a bit frightened, too, of losing the point—or, the bet—or, whatever he wanted her to make with him. She knew that Ross was so much better at these kinds of games than she was. And she'd already lost so much of herself to him already.

"Look, Ross," Rachel said, taking a deep breath, "it's already past time for you to be on your way. I had fun—the kids had fun. So let's just call it a night, okay?"

He shook his head. "Uh-uh. Not yet. Not until I let you prove your point."

"I don't need to prove any point."

"Yes, you do," he said.

"Ross, I'm not going along with this, okay? So just cut it out."

He shifted his weight from one, long, jeans-clad leg to the other and Rachel watched breathlessly. "But, see, if you don't go along with me, then I can't leave."

"You *won't* leave, you mean," she said, glaring at him now.

"Okay, so I won't leave. And then what will your neighbors think? I'm sure they'll be wondering just where and with whom I'm sleeping when I stay over."

"This is a dirty trick, Ross, even for you," Rachel said.

He shrugged. "I like tricks. They can make life interesting. They get results."

She rolled her eyes upward.

"Look, it's not like I'm asking for the world from you."

But he was. He just didn't know it.

"I've heard enough of this, Ross. You've got to go now."

He sobered. "Throw me out."

"You know I can't physically do that."

"Then I guess I'm not leaving."

Rachel sighed heavily. "One kiss, Ross—and then you'll go? Is that a promise?"

He nodded. "Yeah."

She held up her finger to make sure. "Just one kiss."

"Just one," he repeated, so close to her now that the front of his thighs were rubbing against hers. Within a second she felt his manhood pressing against her lower abdomen. He was hot—and hard. Automatically, all the blood in her body rushed to that area.

"Look," she said anxiously, licking her dry lips. "One kiss, okay—but you can't use your hands—or any other parts of your body."

"What?" he said, frowning at her.

"You heard me. No hands. No body parts. Just your lips."

"No tongue, either?"

She shook her head. "No tongue."

"Uh-uh," he replied. "No deal."

"Ross," Rachel said, "you can't have everything your way. It's fifty-fifty—or nothing."

"But you like for me to use my hands. And my tongue," he argued playfully.

Her stomach quivered at the thought. "Well, not this time," she said firmly.

Ross shook his head. "I don't think that you want to play fair."

"And cornering me like this is fair?"

He gazed at her for a moment before a smirky little grin turned up his mouth. "Yeah. It is."

"You're arrogant."

"And you're cute."

Surprisingly, Rachel found that she was now enjoying their banter. It was light, breezy, fun. Sexy. And leading nowhere, he'd promised. She smiled up at him.

And then suddenly Ross took her mouth with the stern determination of a man who had taken all that he could. And he kissed her that way—relentlessly, passionately. He used only his lips as his instrument of seduction until she was so hot for him she thought she would die if he didn't use his hands, his tongue, his whole body, to put out the fire he'd started in her.

And then, just as suddenly, he released her. Flat-out. Just like that. "You lose," he drawled with a gloating smile.

Rachel was stunned by the abrupt ending to his kiss. Leaning back against the wall, she drew in a ragged breath. "You never even gave me a chance," she finally stated.

He stepped back arrogantly. "Did you think I would?"

"Yes, I guess I was naive enough to think that."

"Well, you should've known better."

Rachel drew in another ragged breath. "Yes, I should've." Then she glared at him. "Sometimes, you can almost make me hate you, Ross Murdock."

"Well, don't lose any sleep over it. I've had that same feeling about you at times," he replied.

"Oh," Rachel said in total frustration of his lofty attitude. "You know something, I wouldn't go back to you for ten million dollars."

"Yeah—well..." he said, giving her that cocky grin of his, "that's one of the things I've always admired about you, Rachel. You were never a gold digger."

He turned toward the door to leave, then stopped and looked back. "Just remember, Rachel, after to-night, the next time you try to tell me—or yourself—that you don't want me, we're both going to know that you're lying."

Rachel was so angry, she felt certain that the top of her head was going to lift off like a flying saucer. Glancing down, she saw a throw pillow on the sofa, picked it up and tossed it through the air at him. He dodged, however, easily, and it hit the bookshelf behind him, knocking over a ceramic vase. It crashed to the floor and broke into pieces.

Ross glanced over at her. "Bad shot, Rachel. You need practice."

Rachel glared at him. She thought of picking up another throw pillow and sailing it toward him. But he would have dodged it, too. And then he would have had something more to gloat at.

So, instead of allowing him to get the better of her for even one more second, she turned and stormed down the hallway to her bedroom. She slammed the door shut behind her and threw herself across her bed in the hopes of having herself one long cry.

By golly, she deserved one. She'd earned it.

A few minutes later she heard Ross leave her house.

And then she began to cry.

Chapter Eight

In some ways, the following days passed quickly for Rachel. In other ways, they seemed endless. Ross was in Houston for three of those days. He sent her roses during that time, but she was still so angry with him that she had the delivery boy take them back to the florist. But by the time he'd telephoned from Houston on his third day to say he would be returning to Abbeville that night, Rachel found herself wanting to see him again, in spite of herself.

For several days now she had been waking up in the mornings with nausea that lasted until almost noon, and there was now a tenderness that had developed in her breasts that made them sensitive to even the slightest touch. She couldn't seem to get enough sleep, no matter how many short naps she took during the day. In fact, Jan had taken the boys swimming at a friend's house that very afternoon, and she'd fallen asleep on the sofa and had stayed there the entire time they were gone.

And, of course, there was her late period. That alone was making it more and more difficult to deny that she was pregnant. But it wasn't only that. She had a feeling now...a kind of knowing deep inside her soul that she was carrying Ross's baby.

And yet...even with her most primitive, feminine instincts pointing in that direction, it seemed so unreal to her that she could actually be pregnant. First off, the timing was all wrong. All too soon she would be a single parent, and already she had two strong-willed young sons whom she had raised practically on her own, with little emotional assistance from their father. True, Ross was actively involved in their lives right now, but she didn't think that was going to last much longer.

And the truth of the matter was, she was barely coping with her responsibilities of today. How was she ever going to handle the stress of a divorce and a pregnancy all at the same time?

Rachel frowned. Well, if she was pregnant, then there wasn't anything she could do about it now. At least, not from her standpoint.

But then again, she didn't want to do anything about it. In fact, she wanted his child, regardless of the mess her life was in. Placing her hands over her lower abdomen, she felt for certain in that instant that she could almost sense a small beating heart there. In truth, it would have been easy for her to confirm her suspicions, if she had wanted to...if she had been ready to. But she wasn't. Not yet.

Not quite yet. She needed to get stronger. Stronger in her belief that she had herself and her children heading in the right direction.

Finally, the day of the auction arrived. Ross picked them up early that morning and drove them to the airport. Then he flew them to Houston in his own private airplane.

Rachel had informed Ross when they had been in the process of making their plans for the trip, that she had no intention of going to their home in Houston. She had known that it would have been much too painful an ordeal for her to have walked back into her house for only a short visit. But, of course, she didn't say as much to Ross. That would've made her look much too vulnerable. Instead, she said that she felt that the trip would be less confusing for the boys if it were handled the same as a vacation. Ross went along with the idea, only he didn't bother telling Rachel until they arrived in Houston that he'd made reservations for them at one of the city's oldest, most luxurious hotels and that he would be staying there with them. He'd even reserved a room for their babysitter, Mrs. Jenkins, as well.

"B-but...why?" Rachel asked, dumbfounded.

"Well, because it's going to be less of a hassle for me this way," he replied. "Besides, Rachel, it's a three-bedroom suite, so there's plenty of room for all of us."

Confronted with this news only after they'd landed at the airport and had climbed into a long, white limousine for the drive to downtown Houston, Rachel realized that unless she wanted to make a fuss and disrupt everyone's day, she really had no choice but to go along with Ross's plans. Besides, they were going to be in Houston for only one night. And Ross had

said that it was a three-bedroom suite, for heaven's
sake. There would be plenty of space for all of them.
And it wasn't as if she was afraid that Ross might try
to pressure her into compromising the standards she
had set for herself—and for him—since their separa-
tion. He was pushy, but with the kids along, he could
go only so far, after all.

They finally arrived at the hotel, entered its spa-
cious lobby and found it bustling with late-morning
activity. But the hotel staff recognized Ross immediately and began catering to him and his party as
though they were American royalty.

The granite floors inside the main lobby were buffed
clean and the three, huge, crystal chandeliers that
hung from the steep cathedral ceiling overhead spar-
kled with lights. The dark-stained registration desk
that lined the far wall was a massive structure of
carved wood and was probably seventy-five feet in
length. On either side of the huge desk was a wide,
winding staircase with a stained wood banister that
lead up to a second-story balcony overlooking the
lobby. Rachel had been in this hotel on many occasions in the past, and yet, each time she entered it, its
opulent, ageless beauty reminiscent of a bygone era
always took her breath away.

They rode the elevator up to their suite. Rachel
walked in first and found the interior was decorated in
deep, rich, jewel tones. The master bedroom was done
in emerald green with tapestry drapes with a metallic
gold piping and a matching bedspread. Rachel mentally decided it would be the one that Ross would use.
For herself, she chose the bedroom next door. Its color
scheme was ruby. The two boys would use the bedroom right across the hall from hers. It had twin beds,

which was perfect for them. Everything looked perfect. Even the vases full of fresh exotic flowers that graced at least one table in each room. The larger parlor itself had three such bouquets.

When they'd registered in the hotel, they had learned that Mrs. Jenkins had already checked into her room and was waiting to hear from them. Rachel gave her baby-sitter a quick call and the elderly woman sounded truly delighted to hear her voice again. In fact, her excitement was so great, it brought tears to Rachel's eyes. They made plans for Mrs. Jenkins to join them in their suite in an hour.

When Rachel hung up with her and turned, she saw that Ross was standing with his hands in his pockets at the huge picture window, looking out over downtown Houston. She cleared her throat to get his attention, and he turned slowly in her direction. "I think I'd like to freshen up and rest some before we leave to go to lunch."

"Okay," he said. "The boys are asking me to take them down to the arcade they saw right next door to the hotel. That ought to give you plenty of time."

After they were gone, it wasn't Rachel's intention to lie across her bed and fall asleep. It just sort of happened that way when she decided to rest for a few minutes with her eyes closed. Nonetheless, the next thing she knew, Ross was coaxing her to wake up, and she was telling herself that she couldn't believe that she had actually dozed off like that—again.

He sat on the edge of her bed and studied her face. After a long moment he said, "Rachel, it's time to get up. You've been asleep for over an hour now. Mrs. Jenkins is here and I thought—"

Rachel's eyes opened wide. "Mrs. Jenkins is here— already," she exclaimed. "Well, why didn't someone tell me?" She swung her feet over the side of the bed and sat up right next to Ross.

"Because you were napping so soundly," he replied. "Obviously, you needed the rest." Then, narrowing his eyes, he studied her face once again. "Rachel, are you all right? I mean, you aren't sick, or something, are you?"

"Of course not." Without even realizing it, her hand came to rest on her lower abdomen and a sudden feeling of warmth spread over her.

He looked down her body, and when he saw her hand on her stomach, he placed his on top of it and entwined his fingers with hers. "Do you have a stomach ache?"

Oh—God, Rachel thought, her insides crumbling into pieces all over again. How much of this was she supposed to take without coming completely apart? "No."

"Then why do you have your hand there?"

She could hardly breathe by now without it being an effort. "Just habit, I guess," she replied.

He began to move his hand—and hers—straight down the trunk of her body in a slow, sensuous way until his hand slipped right over the edge of her pelvis and cupped the most feminine part of her body.

This time Rachel's chest totally decompressed itself of oxygen.

A smile eased across Ross's face. But it wasn't cocky or arrogant. It was just a smile, and she wasn't even sure what it meant.

"Ross," she said, holding on to a tight, anxious breath. "The kids and Mrs. Jenkins are in the next room, for heaven's sake."

His grin widened. "I know that."

By now her blood was boiling. So much so, that the tips of her fingers throbbed with a burning need to explore—something—anything—him. She had absolutely no idea how much farther Ross planned to push this little game of his, nor did she know how much more of it she could take. She was only human, after all, and they had already gone past the boundaries she had set for them. They were separated, how many times was she going to have to remind Ross of that fact?

One thing was for sure, though. She wanted him, and he knew it, damn him, anyway.

Suddenly he brought her hand to his mouth and kissed her palm. He never said a word. He never had to. The heat from his gaze was saying it all. He wanted her, too. And he didn't care who knew it.

But she cared. She had her children to consider. She had morals to teach them. And, too, there was the fact that Mrs. Jenkins was in the next room.

Ross stood and walked to the window. "Look," he said, dragging in a deep breath, "how soon can you be ready to leave for the restaurant?"

"Uh . . . Give me fifteen minutes."

"You got it," he replied. Then he turned and walked out, closing her bedroom door behind him.

When Rachel finally made her appearance in the parlor, she and Mrs. Jenkins had only a short re-union before Ross whisked her out the suite door as she was telling the baby-sitter to order room service for herself and the children. By the time they had traveled down the elevator to the lobby, a limousine was already waiting for them at the door.

Within minutes they arrived at the restaurant where Ross had made reservations and were escorted to their table right away. Rachel was famished and was looking forward to the fabulous food she knew this particular restaurant was known to serve. Before long she found herself relaxing and thoroughly enjoying herself.

Ross, she knew, was making it his business to be charming and soon Rachel found herself not wanting to talk about all the bad times in their marriage, but only the good. They reminisced about the old days, going as far back as their high school years when the thrill of falling in love had been so new for them. Rachel laughed at times and blushed at others. Ross was notorious for remembering every little detail about any given subject. He taunted her with the nitty-gritty details of their first time together, and they laughed when remembering how clumsy they had been.

It wasn't until they got ready to order a cocktail before lunch that reality set in and Rachel was forced into recalling the possibility that she was pregnant. She ordered a glass of decaffeinated ice tea instead of the Bloody Mary she would have ordinarily had. Ross didn't seem to notice the switch, and she certainly didn't draw attention to it. She might be ready right now to deal with the fact that she was pregnant with his child, but she wasn't anywhere near being ready to tell him about it. In fact, she didn't even want to have to think about that right now.

During the course of their meal, it came to Ross's attention and, eventually, to hers, as well, that several of his business acquaintances were also dining in the restaurant. One by one, each of them made it a point of stopping by their table to give their regards. There was one acquaintance whom Rachel hadn't ever met, and Ross introduced her as his wife to the very attractive, middle-aged woman.

"Darlene Spielman, this is my wife, Rachel. Rachel, Darlene Spielman. She's the whiz kid with Stan, Liberman and Associates. They're out of Dallas," he explained.

"I see," Rachel replied. And she did. Like Ross, the woman was probably a financial genius. But that wasn't all she was. In fact, it was plain to Rachel that the woman was interested—very interested—in her husband. Her giveaway, Rachel decided, was in the seductive way she looked at Ross. As if she could've eaten him alive, if he'd let her. Anyway, Rachel didn't like it. Not one bit. Darlene Spielman could just go look at some other woman's husband like that. Ross was her property. Maybe she didn't have a right to feel that way. Nonetheless, she did.

But then again, she told herself a moment later, maybe she did still have that right.

Protocol made Rachel extend her hand toward the woman. "How do you do?" she said.

The woman took Rachel's hand and then cut her eyes in Ross's direction. "Why, Ross Murdock," she said in a throaty voice, "you sly fox, you. I didn't know that you had such a lovely wife."

Ross glanced at Rachel and smiled like he could have been appraising her true value for the first time in his life. "Funny, you should walk up and say that, Darlene. 'Cause I was just thinking what a lucky man I am."

A warm, satisfied glow settled over Rachel as she pulled her hand free of the other woman's.

"Indeed," Darlene said, "though I must say, she's a lucky woman, too."

Instinctively, Rachel placed her hand on Ross's arm. He looked at her and smiled, and she smiled back.

Darlene took a step back from their table. "Well," she said, "I guess I should be running along."

"It was nice to meet you, Darlene," Rachel said.

"It was my pleasure, I'm sure," she replied.

And then Darlene Spielman turned with a stiff back and walked away.

Taking a deep, satisfied breath, Rachel removed her hand from Ross's arm and sat back to enjoy the cherry Jubilee that she'd ordered for dessert.

After lunch, Ross and Rachel climbed back into the limousine that awaited them. Ross gave the driver the address where the auction for Kids' Kare was being held. One of Rachel's good friends, Marcelle Le-Blanc was running the shelter these days and she met them at the door.

"Oh, Rachel," she said, "I'm so glad you decided to come."

"Me, too," Rachel replied.

Ross excused himself and walked on ahead.

"So," Marcelle said, turning to Rachel, "when are you coming back to us for good? The shelter needs your help."

"I miss it," Rachel replied. "But I just don't know yet. I may never return to Houston."

"Oh, don't say that," her friend said.

"I'm not saying it. I really don't know just yet what I'm going to do."

"Well...guess what?" Marcelle said, leaning in close. "Just so you'll know, rumor here has it that you'll be going back to Ross soon."

Rachel's eyes widened. "Who would start such a rumor?"

Her friend shrugged. "Beats me."

"Well, that's absurd."

Her friend looked her in the eyes. "Is it, really?"

"Of course," Rachel said, scanning the crowd that was gathering in the room. Her eyes met Ross's and he smiled.

Marcelle touched Rachel on the arm. "Look, honey, I've got to run. They need me in the other room. I'll see you later, okay?"

"Sure," Rachel said with a smile.

Ross strolled up to her almost right away and suggested they take their seats before the auction got under way. Already, the rows were filling up with people who had come expecting to spend large sums of money in the name of charity. Some of them wore designer clothes. Others were more moderately dressed. Rachel was dressed in a soft pink tailored suit and pearls and looked exquisitely fashioned for the occasion. Ross was wearing navy trousers and a light gray sports jacket. They made a handsome couple and Ross never left Rachel's side during the entire function. It turned into one of those nice, cozy afternoons like the ones they'd once had years ago.

The auction ended up being quite successful, making enough money to keep the children's shelter up and running smoothly for some time to come. On their way back to the hotel, Ross had the limousine driver take them by a candy shop that had always been one of Rachel's favorites. Ross went inside and came back out with a heart-shaped box of chocolates. He climbed in the limousine and gave it to Rachel. "I know it's not Valentine's Day, but then again, it doesn't have to be, now does it?"

"No," Rachel said, her heart pounding to the rhythm of some wild, crazy beat. Moroccan, she thought. "Thank you," she said, leaning over and kissing him on the cheek. "That was sweet of you."

He grinned and then told the driver of the limo to take them back to their hotel now. They gave Mrs. Jenkins the rest of the day off, and the kindly woman went back to her room on a lower floor.

The children were getting restless from being inside and Ross promised them a trip to Astro-World later that evening when the sun went down. In the meantime, they all decided to go to the private pool provided for them on the same floor as their suite.

Rachel had brought along her bikini bathing suit just in case, and it got her a catcall and the sexiest look from Ross when she walked out of her bedroom. Thank goodness the kids had been standing right there, because no telling what else he would've tried giving her—and no telling what she would've accepted from him. Ross was a good-looking man at all times. In a swimsuit, he was dynamite. It took her breath away to look at him. So she tried not to, but how could she not look at him, when he was the man she loved?

Ross dove into the water with the boys, but Rachel chose to just sit on the side and watch them. She laughed at their competitive games and was quite satisfied to remain where she was until it would be time to go back to their suite.

After a while, Ross got out of the pool and started walking toward her. She told herself not to watch him, that it was simply an urge in her to do so, not a necessity.

He reached her, and Rachel finally looked up and handed him a towel. He took it from her and began rubbing the excess moisture from his hair.

Then, suddenly he tossed the towel to the side, like he had no real use for it, bent down and, in one split second, lifted Rachel from her chair. It all happened so fast that she didn't even have time to protest.

Her heart slammed against her breastbone.

"Ross..." she squealed, now that her breath had returned to her. "Don't you dare do this... Don't you dare throw me in."

But he only grinned at her like he couldn't hear a word she was saying, and in less time than it took to swat a fly, he tossed her out over the water. She seemed to hang there momentarily like a weightless feather and then began her descent like a flagging albatross.

And then *splash!* It was all over with and she was under the water and fighting to come up for air.

She broke through the surface spluttering and coughing—and, obviously, was one of the most hilarious things her husband and children had seen in a long time. "I'll get you for this, Ross Murdock," she threatened. "Just you wait and see."

That remark seemed to bring on an even larger bout of laughter from them.

The first person she saw when she was able to see clearly again was Danny. His bottom lip was trembling.

"You're not mad at Daddy, are you?"

Of course she was. She was furious with Ross. But then, she couldn't very well tell Danny that and have him burst into tears. "No, Danny. I'm not mad at him."

Jorgie swam up to them. "My friend Kurt says that when his mommy and daddy get mad at each other, they say, *Let's kiss and make up.* So that's what you and Daddy need to do. Kiss and make up."

By this time, Ross had swum up to them. "Now, that's not a bad idea, Jorgie." He looked at Rachel. "What do you say, my little drenched kitty, wanna give it a try?"

Drenched kitty, indeed. The nerve of him.

"I—I already told Danny that I wasn't mad at you," she stammered, defensively.

"Please, Mommy, kiss Daddy," Danny said.

"Yeah. Just kiss him," Jorgie added.

Rachel glared at Ross.

He shrugged playfully. "Hey, what can I say? I'm just a kissable guy, I guess."

Yeah—right. And she was the Princess of Troy.

"Come on, Mommy," Jorgie insisted. "Just kiss him." Rachel looked at her son for a moment and realized that her son knew exactly what he was doing. He may have been only eight years old, but he was a cunning eight-year-old, that was for sure.

Like father, like son, she thought to herself.

"Okay," she said pleasantly, like it was going to be no big deal for her. But kissing Ross at any time, in any fashion, was always a big deal for her. She turned her face up to his and a moment later his lips touched hers.

It was that quick. That simple. And then it was over.

And it really hadn't been such a big deal for her. At least, her kids were happy now.

She was smiling at them when a second later Ross dunked her under water. "You're it, Rachel," he yelled back at her from over his shoulder as he swam off in the other direction. The kids squealed with laughter.

Rachel came up spluttering and coughing, again. When finally her lungs were clear, she slicked back her bangs from her face and targeted Ross with her eyes like torpedoes. "Let's get him, boys," she said, and Jorgie and Danny swam off along with her to help their mother avenge her honor against the pirate prince. They played that game until the boys grew tired and chose to simply float around on their tubes in the shallow water. Rachel swam off on her back toward the deeper end. The cool water on her skin felt wonderfully refreshing to her. She felt clean... fresh... almost slick to the touch.

Suddenly, Ross was swimming under her and before she could swim away, he pulled her down under the water with him. Then, almost as quickly, he let her go and she came back up for air. She took a deep breath and then found herself being thoroughly kissed.

She couldn't fight him. She couldn't even breathe. Ross's hands were everywhere on her skin. She clung to him. He was her life support and her drowning bed. And just when she thought her lungs would explode, he released her.

It took several moments before Rachel could speak; she was so angry with Ross. "Why did you do that?" she asked accusingly, breathlessly.

He grinned. "'Cause you're my wife and I wanted to."

"I'm not your wife anymore," Rachel said, breathing hard. "Not really. We don't live together, anymore, remember?"

"Oh, yeah, that's true. We just sleep together, right, when it's at your convenience?"

Rachel gaped open-mouthed at him.

"I'm going to the room," she finally said.

"Fine. So am I," he replied. He looked back over his shoulder. "Let's go, guys. Time to get ready to go to Astro-World."

In spite of everything, Ross and Rachel were able to put aside their differences for their children's sake, and Astro-World was a lot of fun. By the time they got back to the hotel that night it was after midnight and Rachel was exhausted. Ross helped her to get the kids into bed. When she announced to him that she was going to bed, he didn't protest. He went into the parlor and fixed himself a nightcap.

Rachel awoke the following morning to the smell of coffee brewing. The aroma seeped in through her nostrils and nausea descended upon her empty stomach like a tidal wave. It sent her rolling out of bed in a hurry with her hand over her mouth. She barely made it to the bathroom in time. Like clockwork, her morning sickness had come again.

She didn't hear Ross enter her bedroom. She saw him only when he reached the doorway leading into the bathroom.

"What's wrong?" he asked, his eyebrows deepening into a frown.

"Nothing," she finally replied.

He handed her a dampened washcloth. "You're throwing up and there's nothing wrong? That's ridiculous."

She got sick, again, and he waited for her to finish. "Something's wrong, Rachel. What is it?"

She wiped her face with the washcloth. "I must have caught a virus, or something."

"A virus—or perhaps you ate a bad chili dog last night," he commented.

That remark renewed Rachel's need to vomit.

"I'm calling a doctor," he said a moment later.

"No. No, doctor," she said, shaking her head. "I don't need one. I'll be fine in a minute."

She straightened and took in a slow, deep breath. "I think I'll go back to bed for a while."

He swooped her up into his arms, carried her to the mattress and laid her down. "The kids are up, so I'll close the door so that you can sleep."

She nodded and closed her eyes.

"Rachel?"

She opened them. "What?"

He was frowning down at her in concern.

"Are you certain that you're all right? I mean, you're not hiding an illness of some kind from me, are you?"

She shut her eyes. "No, Ross. I don't have an illness that I'm hiding from you."

He released a heavy sigh. "Well, that's sure good to know."

Chapter Nine

Flying them home that day, Ross watched Rachel more closely than he did the instrument panel in front of him. But he had no reason to worry about her. She was doing fine, now that her morning bout with nausea had finally passed, and, by the time they landed in Louisiana, she was almost sorry their trip was completed. Now it was back to reality for her—and time once again to draw the line that would knowingly separate Ross's world from hers.

And yet, as if she didn't have enough to worry about already, there was a very definite part of her that no longer wanted to be separated from him. Quite frankly, it scared the heck out of her to discover she was no longer sure how to make a better life for herself and her children. It had taken only one lousy weekend with Ross in Houston for that part of her to become a complete traitor. It was sickening.

She was such a weak person. Like her mother had been.

Somehow, some way, she would have to find a way to reunite her defenses against Ross.

From the airport, Ross drove them back to Rachel's house, and she was the first one to get out of his car and hurry down the walkway. She unlocked the front door and soon Ross entered with a suitcase in each hand. "Where do you want these?" he asked.

"The blue one goes in the boys' room and the beige one goes in mine," Rachel shot back from over her shoulder. He disappeared for a few moments and then returned empty-handed. She was waiting for him. "Thank you, Ross, for everything—the weekend was great. You made certain that the kids and I enjoyed ourselves, and we did."

Jorgie and Danny walked up and Ross hugged them against him. "I had a good time, too. We'll do it again, soon, okay? Certainly before school starts."

"Yeah!" Jorgie and Danny exclaimed at the same time.

Rachel expected Ross to leave now.

He didn't.

The kids went out to the backyard to see if they could find Jorgie's king snake again. And Rachel just stood there, waiting for him to make a move, but it didn't seem as though he was in any big hurry.

Finally she turned and went into the kitchen. "I need a glass of water," she said. In truth, she needed something right then. A break would have helped.

"Yeah," Ross replied, following right on her heels. I could use one, too." She poured a glassful and gave it to him. He gulped it down and placed the empty glass near the sink.

Then he turned to her and blocked her path from walking away had she chosen to.

Oh, God, Rachel thought suddenly, her pulses racing, what was he going to do now?

He grinned.

She blushed—because she knew he had read her thoughts.

He laughed. "You really don't trust me, do you? What do you think I'm going to do? Eat you up like a big, bad wolf?"

Rachel's blush deepened. Ross had always presented a sense of danger for her. The kind of danger that always tantalized her sensibilities to excess and always, always made her want to come back to him for more.

"Look," he said, "I have but one purpose in mind at the moment and that's to tell you something."

Rachel had been holding tight to her breath, but now she released it. "What do you want to say?"

He took a deep breath. "Well, I didn't want to say anything to you before now because I was afraid it would've ended up spoiling the weekend for us."

Rachel's heart started pounding. She had no idea what he was going to say, but the look in his eyes was so serious, so heartfelt, that it alarmed her. "What is it?"

He exhaled heavily. "Look, here's the deal," he went on. "I'm going to have to go out of the country for a week—possibly as long as ten days. I know I practically promised you that I wouldn't go away anymore on long business trips, but this is something that's been in the planning stages for months now. I didn't expect it to come to the bargaining table so soon, and, to put it quite frankly, my two new assistants simply aren't ready yet to take on this kind of project all by themselves. I'm going to have to go along with them."

She had known that he would leave them again, sooner or later. So why, then, wasn't she better prepared for the moment?

Rachel struggled to keep control of her emotions. Inwardly, she was a mess. Outwardly, she gave him a careless shrug. "You don't owe me an explanation for your actions, Ross. Not anymore."

"Well, I happen to think I do. Besides, I want you to understand that sometimes there are going to be certain situations that will come up in my business affairs that I'll simply have to take care of myself. But I don't want you to feel threatened by that. Because there's no reason for you to. You and the kids come first with me now—and that will never, ever change."

If only Rachel could've believed that. Even for a moment.

A part of her did.

But the rest of her didn't.

She frowned.

Taking her by the shoulders, Ross gazed into her eyes. "Look, we had a great weekend together with the kids. Let's not let this spoil it for us, okay?"

Rachel knew she had to get a grip on herself.

"It was really a nice weekend," she said.

"It was perfect," he replied.

"Mmm, maybe. When are you leaving?"

Before answering her, he took a step back and released a deep breath. "That's the kicker. First thing in the morning," he said.

"Ten days, you say."

"Yeah. I'll be meeting with several investors over that period of time. One of them lives on this island just off the northeast coast of South America. He's a recluse—or so I've heard—and doesn't like people very much. So I don't know how long it's going to take me to deal with him."

Rachel smiled. "Well, I'm sure if anyone can handle him, you can. Will you call?" she asked, suddenly gazing up at him.

"Actually," he said, looking deep into her eyes, "I thought that you might not want me to."

Ten whole days without hearing from him?

An eternity—or so it seemed to her at the moment.

"Well, maybe you should," she said. "That way I can give you news of the boys—and they could talk to you. I know they'd like that."

"Yeah, you're right," he said. "I'll call."

When? Rachel thought to herself.

"Good," she replied, smiling at him.

He stepped back then. "I guess I'd better go outside and tell the kids goodbye. I'll be right back."

Rachel nodded.

"So wait right here for me, okay?"

"Okay. I will."

Ross went out the back door and Rachel stayed where she was and watched him through the window. Dropping down to his sons' height, he spoke to them for several minutes before he stood again and started back toward the house.

Rachel's heart began to pound in her throat.

He stepped through the back door, stopped and looked at her from that distance away. Then suddenly his long strides ate up the distance separating them, and, without saying a word, he pulled Rachel into his arms and kissed her passionately on the mouth.

Then he released her, turned around and walked out.

The next two days passed without any word from Ross, but Rachel really hadn't expected him to call so soon, so that was okay. A part of her had just hoped that he would have.

She awakened on the morning of the third day knowing that after she put her children to bed that night, she was going to go into the privacy of her bathroom and take the pregnancy test she'd purchased for herself at the drugstore. After all, it was time to do something. Her symptoms hadn't subsided. If anything, they were increasing in their intensity. It was time she knew for sure if she was carrying Ross's child.

That night, after the boys were asleep, Rachel walked into her bathroom and quietly closed the door behind her. She reached for the box she'd placed on the top shelf, opened it and read the directions inside. Three times, in fact, just to make sure. She was so nervous about taking the test, she wanted to make sure she understood the instructions completely. The last thing she wanted to do at this point was make a mistake.

She followed the directions down to the final detail and then waited the allotted time before checking the results. When she saw by the color code that she was, indeed, pregnant, she grew weak all over.

And then a moment later she was crying and laughing—almost giddy in her excitement. She had known she was pregnant all along.

There were so many things for her to consider now. So many things to reconsider. She was going to have a baby, for heaven's sake. Ross's baby.

Then, suddenly, from out of nowhere, some spoil-sport part of her held up a red light right in front of her face. *Hold it, Rachel,* it said. *Have you lost your mind? How can you be so thrilled about this baby when you aren't planning to have a husband for much longer?*

That was one of the things that Rachel knew she had to think about—at some point. But not tonight. Tonight belonged to her—and to the very beginnings of the new life within her. How could she not want to feel special about being pregnant with this baby, if only for a little while? For Rachel, this was what being a woman was all about, and nothing she would do in her lifetime would ever compare to giving life to her children. Nothing. Not ever. No matter what she did.

Rachel drew herself a tub of warm water, added a few drops of her favorite perfume oil and took a long, leisurely soak. And while she lay in the cozy cocoon of her bathtub, allowing her mind to drift, she thought of the child she'd miscarried just last year and took a moment to pray. Oh, please, God, she whispered in the silence of her heart, let me carry my baby to full term and then let him or her be born into the world as healthy and as strong as Jorgie and Danny were. Oh, please . . .

And maybe it was simply wishful thinking on her part, but somewhere, deep down inside, Rachel honestly believed that her prayers for her unborn child had been heard and were already being answered. Once again, she allowed her mind to drift across the miles of time, through the yesterdays of loving Ross. Did she really want to live out all of her tomorrows without him?

The answer, of course, was no. But it was necessary, wasn't it? She couldn't trust him again, could she?

Certainly, at one time she had felt that way. But Ross had changed since then, she was just afraid to admit that to herself. Now with another baby on the way... What if Jan was right? What if he had really changed for good this time? Did she dare take the chance that he had?

In truth, she was finding that she really wanted to. And it wasn't just the kids... or the child she carried. It was her own need for him, too. She loved him. She always would. If there was even the slightest chance that he'd meant what he'd said...

Rachel's heart began to pound. Maybe there was hope for them, after all....

During the next three days Rachel's telephone seemed to be ringing constantly, and each time it did, she found herself almost breaking her neck to get it. Sometimes it was a telemarketing person on the other end trying to sell her something. A few times it was Jan. But, never, ever was it the voice of the person she wanted so desperately to hear from. But he'd said he would call, and she believed he would. When he had time, of course.

And then on the sixth day after Ross's departure out of the country on business, Rachel picked up the ringing telephone and heard the overseas operator at the other end of the line. Her heart jumped into her throat.

As soon as the boys understood that it was their father on the phone, they were at Rachel's side in a heartbeat and she allowed them to talk to Ross first so that when her time came, she would be able to speak to him without being interrupted.

"Hi, again," he said, when at last she got the receiver back from Danny.

There was the usual overseas pause after he'd spoken.

"Hi, yourself," she replied, her heart still pounding with excitement. She had been so afraid that his call might have gotten disconnected or something before she had gotten her turn to talk to him.

"Are you and the kids all right?" he asked.

"Yes, we're fine. How about you?"

"Fine. Just fine. Listen, I want you, Jorgie and Danny to do me a big favor. I only have one more investor left to meet with, and he's the recluse I told you about. Anyway, I'll be coming back to the States in two days. I'd like for the three of you to meet me in Miami. We can fly to the Keys for a few days and spend a little time relaxing on the beach. What do you say? Will you come?"

He sounded so hopeful, in spite of the fact that she could barely hear him.

And she missed him so much.

And so did the boys, she knew.

And the Florida Keys might just turn out to be the perfect place for her to tell him the shocking news that he was going to be a father, again—and that . . . well, and that she was thinking now about giving their marriage another chance.

"Yes. The boys and I will come to meet you. But where? At the same hotel we've stayed in the past?"

"Yes. Meet me there in two days."

"We will," Rachel assured him the moment she knew he could hear her.

There was the usual pause, but just when Rachel was certain he was going to speak again, the phone lines went completely dead.

Tears of frustration sprang into her eyes. She held the receiver to her ear and listened to the empty sound of the disconnected line. Finally, she took a deep breath and replaced it on its base.

And then she realized that she would be seeing him in two days and her spirits lifted. She went in search of her children to tell them about the upcoming trip.

Rachel called a travel agency within the hour and by that afternoon her travel arrangements were secure. The following day she packed a suitcase for each of them. Then she drove by Jan's apartment for a visit to let her sister know that she and the kids were leaving town the following morning.

Bright and early the next day, in spite of the nausea that made her want to remain in bed just a bit longer, Rachel got up, called a cab and she and the boys went to the airport and boarded their flight.

They landed at the Miami airport before noon and went straight to their hotel. Rachel spent the afternoon entertaining her children while waiting for Ross. When Ross didn't show up by nightfall, she began to get worried and checked with the front desk to make certain she didn't have a message from him. When he still hadn't arrived later that night, she became frantic and stayed up until dawn watching the weather channel, the news channel, until finally, she couldn't take anymore and she called the local authorities. By breakfast, she still didn't know anything more about his whereabouts.

Now she was really frantic. But she tried not to show it because of the children.

Eventually it dawned on her to call Ross's office in Houston. If anyone would know his whereabouts, it would be his lifelong secretary, Norma Whetting. But Miami time was an hour ahead, so his office wasn't open yet. Rachel made a quick decision to call the older woman at her home. She was certain Mrs. Whetting wouldn't mind.

And she didn't. She told Rachel that the last conversation she'd had with anyone from Ross's party was yesterday morning when one of the two young assistant brokers traveling with him phoned to say that Ross had left them on the mainland to travel to this private island to meet with an investor. Anyway, Ross hadn't returned that night and the young assistants felt certain that due to stormy weather conditions, he had probably been invited to stay over on the island until the deal was finalized.

"So, you see," Mrs. Whetting went on to assure Rachel, "there's absolutely nothing for you to be worried about. Mr. Murdock is just being Mr. Murdock. You know how he is. It's always business before pleasure for him. I'm sure he'll join you and the boys as soon as he closes that deal."

No doubt, Rachel thought. But, dammit, she wasn't going to be here waiting for him when he decided to show up. She'd already been through this with him too many times in the past.

She thanked Mrs. Whetting for her help and hung up. Then she called the airport and scheduled an early afternoon flight home.

She had known all along, she told herself as she packed to leave, that the minute she was no longer a challenge for Ross, he would lose interest in her. She was a fool for having convinced herself otherwise.

Actually, she thought, someone needed to give him an Academy Award for his devious performance as a changed man. He'd earned it. He'd acted out his part so well that he'd had her completely convinced.

Then he'd snatched that newfound trust right out from under her.

Well, that was all right. She didn't need him anyway.

Liar.

She called a cab to pick them up from the hotel and take them to the airport, and then she checked out of their room. By the time she and the boys reached the airport it was almost noon and the weather outside was oppressively hot. Rachel took her sons by the hand and hurried them inside. Finding the direction she needed to go, she pulled them along. They went down one corridor, took a right and then rushed down the next one. They were about to make another turn when Rachel heard someone calling her name and she glanced back over her shoulder.

And that's when she saw him—Ross—coming toward her and the kids. His beard was stubbled and he looked as though he hadn't changed his clothes in a couple of days. In fact, he looked haggard—and yet, perfect. Only this time, considering his appearance, his die-hard motto of business before pleasure had taken its toll on him. Well, it had cost her, too. Plenty.

He was glaring in her direction as he swerved through the crowd that separated them.

When he reached her, he jerked the carry-on bag she was carrying off her shoulder. "Where in the hell are you going?'' he asked. He was right in her face—and angry.

Well, she was angry, too.

''Home.''

''Like hell, you are. I just got here.''

''I can see that.''

His hands went to his hips. ''Damn you, Rachel. Why didn't you wait for me at the hotel like you said you would?''

''I did wait. You didn't show up. Nor did you bother to call.''

''I would've, dammit, except that there wasn't a telephone in working order on the island where I got stranded.''

Rachel smirked. ''That's a good one, Ross, even for you.''

''It's true, dammit!''

A sudden weakness enveloped Rachel at the possibility that he was actually telling her the truth, and she placed her hand on Jorgie's shoulder for support. ''I don't believe it.''

''Of course, you don't,'' he said sarcastically. ''You never believe anything I say.''

''You could've at least found a telephone to call me.''

''You're not listening to me, Rachel. A storm came up suddenly and I was stranded on this island, for heaven's sake. Power lines were down. The one boat, capable of getting me back to the mainland was damaged. There was nothing I could do. In fact, I got here as fast as I could, but obviously not fast enough for you.''

''Ross,'' Rachel said, her eyes widening, ''I thought—''

"I know exactly what you thought," he said, practically baring his teeth at her. "But this time, lady, you were dead wrong about me."

The room began to swirl before Rachel's eyes. "I—I'm sorry," she stammered.

And then, without any more warning than that, everything went black for her.

When Rachel woke up, she was on a stretcher in an ambulance and was being rushed to a hospital. She was assured that her children were safe with their father and that they were going to meet her there. Rachel insisted to the paramedic on board that she didn't need to go to the emergency room because she already knew what was wrong with her. But her words fell on deaf ears, and soon she was in the examining room of a local hospital.

A doctor came in, and, of course, Rachel didn't have any choice but to tell him that she was pregnant. He ordered a series of blood tests for her and then walked away before Rachel could warn him to keep her condition confidential—even from her husband. She told a nurse that she needed to see the doctor that had examined her right away and the nurse assured Rachel that she would find him for her. Then she, too, disappeared. And so now Rachel waited—anxiously—for one of them to return. If it hadn't been for the fact that she was still feeling a bit woozy, she would've gotten up herself and gone to find him.

In the meantime, Ross sat with his sons in the waiting area, anxiously waiting for someone to come forward to give him news about Rachel's condition.

He still couldn't believe that she had just fainted like that. It was all his fault. He couldn't believe he had been such a heel. He had been so angry at her for not waiting for him. He had wanted so desperately to explain to her what had happened to him, that when he'd telephoned the hotel the moment he'd landed in Miami and found out she'd just checked out of her room, he'd lost his mind. But he had been wrong, and he knew that now.

"Mr. Murdock?"

Pulling back his outstretched legs, Ross glanced up quickly. "Uh, yes, Doctor, what is it?" He stood, then automatically looked back over his shoulder to make sure that his sons were still sitting where they had been only moments ago. They were.

The doctor looked at him from over the rim of his glasses. "You are Mr. Murdock, Rachel Murdock's husband, am I correct?"

Pulses racing, Ross nodded his head. "That's right."

The doctor cleared his throat. "About your wife's condition, I was wondering—"

"Her condition?" Ross cut in. He pulled his eyebrows together in a frown. "What condition are you talking about?"

"Well, first off, she's anemic and—"

"She is?" Ross replied in concern. "That can be serious sometimes, can't it?"

"Yes, that's correct. In fact, it can be very serious for a woman when she's pregnant—as is your wife's case."

Ross's frown deepened. "My wife's case? What are you trying to say, Doc? Is my wife pregnant?"

The doctor paused with a frown on his face. "Oh, my. Hasn't she told you yet?"

Ross felt like someone had just punched him in the stomach. He remembered that time in Houston when

Rachel had gotten sick to her stomach. He'd blamed it on the chili dog she'd eaten. She'd said it was a virus. But, in truth, she had known all along what the actual cause was, and she hadn't even told him.

Clenching his jaw tight, Ross smirked.

Damn her, anyway. Just who in hell did Rachel think she was, anyway, keeping him in the dark about his own kid?

In truth, she hadn't given him even an ounce of credit for all he'd done over the last weeks to make up for his past mistakes.

Well at least now he knew what she really thought of him.

And it damned sure wasn't much.

Chapter Ten

The flight home from Miami was a long, nerve-racking one for both Rachel and Ross. They barely spoke, and when they did, it was seldom to each other and only when it was absolutely necessary. Danny sat with Rachel in the front row of the first-class section, and Jorgie sat with his father across the aisle from them.

Ross was furious with her, Rachel knew, for not telling him about the baby and allowing him to find out about it from a complete stranger. He wasn't talking to her at all. In fact, he wouldn't even look at her.

She had tried to tell him that she was sorry, but it seemed that in the short span of a couple of hours, they had switched roles in life. Now, suddenly, he was the one not wanting to listen to reason. And for the first time ever, Rachel was beginning to realize how truly frustrated he must have been with her during the past weeks.

If ever he tried to talk to her again, she would listen.

But from the looks of things, there was a fat chance of that ever happening now. He seemed as though he couldn't wait to get her and the boys back to Lafayette so that he could be rid of her and not have to see her face again. The boys had sensed something had gone wrong between their parents. They were unusually quiet and had not asked many questions concerning their sudden change in plans.

Rachel's heart was in pieces, and she wished that she had someplace where she could go and have herself a good cry.

But there were the children to consider. And so she sat there and pretended to be all right, even though the exact opposite was true.

Ross was thoroughly angry and upset with Rachel. But in spite of all that, his heart was aching. He had thought the worst day of his life had been when Rachel had walked out on him. But now he knew better. At least back then he'd had the hope that he'd get her to come back to him. Now he didn't know if he wanted her back. The fact that she had so little faith in him had wounded him deeply. He didn't know if he'd ever heal. In fact, he felt certain that he wouldn't.

After they landed at the Lafayette airport, he rented a taxi for the twenty-mile ride to Abbeville. When they arrived at Rachel's house, he carried their luggage inside and then asked the two kids to go to their room for a while. They obeyed him immediately.

Then he waited until their bedroom door was closed before turning in Rachel's direction. "Are you still planning to file for a divorce?"

Rachel sucked in a harsh-sounding breath. "W-well, I don't know. Why?"

"I won't protest it if you do. Work out a settlement, and I'll sign it."

"I see," she said, glancing down at the floor.

"But I want joint custody of the kids."

Obviously surprised, Rachel covered her mouth with her hands and then glanced off to the side. For an instant he felt a moment of triumph, but then he thought he saw tears in her eyes and his gut knotted. But in the next moment he decided he wasn't going to worry about her feelings anymore. After all, she didn't worry about his. And, besides, she wanted a divorce from him. He was just giving her what she wanted.

"Uh, Ross," she murmured, and for the first time since they'd left the hospital in Miami he noticed how dark the circles under her eyes were in comparison to her pale complexion, and it jolted him. "Look, do you suppose we could discuss this at another time. I'm simply not up to it right now," she said.

He stepped forward. He thought fleetingly of taking her into his arms. He wanted to more than anything. But maybe it was better to end it quickly— swiftly—before the pain was unbearable. He frowned. "Yeah, sure," he said. "We can do it another time. In fact, why don't I just tell my attorney to get in touch with yours?"

She dropped her eyes to the floor and nodded.

Ross frowned. He had known she wouldn't object. And the part of him that had still hoped that she would . . . well . . . it was a fool.

He turned away, gathered his pride and walked out.

The next few days were tough ones for Rachel. She was thankful that she had her children to keep her going, and slowly she began to pull herself back together. The one good thing about falling completely apart was, once she had the courage to pick up the pieces again and glue them back together, she felt like a whole new person. She no longer doubted her own strength, and that alone gave her the ability to look her fears straight in the eye and defeat them. She was in control of her life and a weight had been lifted from her shoulders.

It was now so easy for her to see that she had been wrong. Ross wasn't anything like her father. Her father had been a cold, self-centered man who hadn't cared for anyone but himself. He'd never looked back once in remorse for the pain he'd caused his wife and children.

But Ross had. He'd had the courage—and the heart—to look back and see the sufferings he'd caused his family. Then he'd done everything within his power to heal the wounds, regardless of how hard she'd fought against his every effort. And now she would do anything, absolutely anything if he would give her a chance to tell him as much.

In fact, maybe it was time that she take matters into her own hands. Jorgie's birthday was on Friday and she was planning to give him a birthday party and invite all his friends from the neighborhood. He'd asked if his father was coming. Unknowingly, Jorgie had given her the perfect excuse to call Ross. Because, surely if Ross knew that Jorgie wanted him at his birthday party, he would come, in spite of his feelings toward her.

It had been a week now since Ross had stormed out of Rachel's house. He'd returned to Houston right away and thrown himself back into his job. He had thought it would appease this ache in him, only it hadn't. He knew now that nothing would—nothing except having his family back. But a marriage between him and Rachel would never work. She didn't have any faith in him, and he couldn't live with her like that.

In some ways, he didn't really blame her. After all, he'd neglected her needs for so many years that it was inevitable that she would end up not having any faith in him. He had thought that he could win her back, but he had been wrong. So now he would have to pay the price for his mistakes. It was that simple.

His secretary buzzed him on the intercom. "Mr. Murdock, your wife is on line two."

His heart jumped in his throat. "Rachel?"

"That's right, sir. Line two."

"Thank you," he replied, leaning forward in his seat. It creaked loudly as his weight shifted. Then, taking a deep breath, he lifted the receiver and then paused momentarily to calm his racing heart. "This is Murdock," he finally responded.

"Ross..."

"Hello, Rachel."

"I hope I'm not disturbing you," she said anxiously.

He was so glad to hear her voice again. "No, no, as a matter of fact, I was just thinking about you."

"I haven't heard from your attorney yet," she said.

"I haven't heard from yours, either."

"I haven't contacted mine," she replied softly.

"Well, I haven't contacted mine, either," he replied.

"Oh," she commented.

"How are the kids? And the baby?" Ross asked.

"Fine. They're all fine."

"And you?"

"Doing well, thank you," Rachel replied.

"Good."

There was a long pause.

Rachel cleared her throat. "Ross, I, uh, I wanted to remind you that it's Jorgie's birthday on Friday and to let you know that I'm giving him a party that afternoon at three o'clock. I've even got this clown that Jan knows coming as entertainment. It should be a lot of fun for the kids. Anyway," she said, and Ross heard when she took a deep breath, "Jorgie asked if you would come for the party. Will you?"

"He wants me to come?"

"Yes, he does," she replied.

"Then, I'll come."

"Good."

Another pause.

"Ross..."

"Yeah," he said, his heart jumping into high gear, which was quite a feat considering it was all broken up.

"I just want you to know that I made a mistake about you. And I'm sorry. Very sorry."

"I see," he replied, holding on to his pride.

"Yes," she replied softly, and Ross was suddenly tempted to just throw his stupid pride away and tell her how he really felt. But then, how could he just fall at her feet like that, when she'd hurt him so badly?

"Well," she said a moment later, "I—I just wanted you to know how I felt about all that happened recently."

"Uh, look," Ross said, trying to make some sense of his own crazy feelings, "I'll see you on Friday. We'll talk then, okay?"

"Oh . . . yes," she replied. "I'd like that very much. On Friday, then."

She hung up.

Ross leaned back in his chair and just stared at the telephone for a long time. Then he remembered something and opened the top right-hand drawer of his desk. From inside, he removed the eight-by-ten photograph of his wife that he'd placed in there a week ago. For several long, thoughtful moments he studied her features. Then he placed the photograph on his desk where it had once stood next to the one of his children and swiveled his chair around until he was staring out his window into nothingness. Taking a deep breath, he closed his eyes. Slowly, a smile eased across his face.

Rachel had called him—and just like that he was ready to forgive her. Lord knew, if she could humble herself enough to forgive him, what right did he have not to forgive her? Actually, he now realized that he had been waiting for just any little old excuse to do just that. And now that he had one, his whole world was turning topsy-turvy.

You're nothing but a pushover, Murdock, a little voice inside told him. *And you're correct. Forgiveness is a two-way street. Besides, it's time you admit the truth to yourself. You're never going to be happy in this life unless you have Rachel at your side. So she hurt your pride. It brought you down to size, didn't it?*

Actually, you ought to thank her. Better yet, why don't you just take her into your arms and kiss her until the pain goes away? Hey, I don't know about you, but I think it would work for me.

Ross opened his eyes, and then a moment later, shot up from his chair. It would work for him, too, by golly. In fact, it was the only thing that could.

He glanced at his Rolex watch, then picked up the telephone and dialed Jan's number. "Jan," he said, "it's Ross. I need your help with something. Are you game?"

"Does it have to do with making up with my sister?"

"It sure does."

"Then I'm game."

By Friday afternoon, Rachel was a nervous wreck. She hadn't heard from Ross again, and she could only assume that he was still coming to Jorgie's birthday party. Rachel just didn't know when. And that's what had her so anxious. She found herself looking up at every sound, hoping it would be him. She was being ridiculous. He hadn't given her any reason for that much hope. He had just said they would talk. But it was a start, and at this point, she held on to anything she could. She loved him, and she needed him. Surely if he had once wanted her back as much as he had claimed, he would somehow find it in his heart to forgive her mistakes. How else would they ever heal each other's wounds?

Jan arrived early to help her set up the backyard for the party. Rachel found her sister to be in an exceptionally good mood, and it helped to make the time pass quicker.

Then children started to arrive and even with Jan's help, Rachel could barely keep up with a backyard full of five-to-eight-year-old children made up mostly of boys who had more energy than a colony of ants. She was so busy in fact that when she bent over to pick up a few party favors one of the children had dropped on the ground, she was startled out of her wits when, suddenly, she heard a loud, old-fashioned bicycle horn blow right next to her ear. She straightened in surprise, turned and saw the clown that she'd hired for the party standing right behind her. He blew his horn at her again in a greeting.

Rachel smiled. "Hi."

Grinning from ear to ear, he honked twice more.

The clown was okay, but that horn of his had to go. It was probably just her luck, though, to have hired a clown to entertain the kids who communicated through a horn.

She looked around for Jan and saw she was busy breaking up an argument between two boys. "Look, there's Jan," she said. "I know the two of you are friends, so why don't you say hello?"

With that, Rachel turned and hurried off to see why one of the children—the little girl from two doors down—was crying and pointing her finger at another child—the little boy from four doors down. It truly looked like it was going to be one of those parties...

Rachel listened to both sides of the children's argument, then gave the little girl back her party hat and gave the boy one of his own. Then she turned around to check on something—she couldn't remember what—and ran right smack-dab into the clown again. She gave him a frown. He gave her a wink.

A wink, mind you.

She'd hired a clown for her eight-year-old son's birthday party who was nothing but a lousy flirt.

She decided that it was time she introduced herself as the hostess. She would have thought he would have figured that out by now, but obviously he hadn't.

She extended her hand out to him. "Hi, I'm Rachel Murdock. You must be Stan, the guy I spoke to over the telephone."

In response to that, the clown honked his horn. Twice.

"Stan is a mimic," Jan explained to her as she walked over to them.

"Oh, I see," Rachel replied. Looking up, her eyes met Stan's, and something held her there for a moment longer than she had intended. A moment too long. She suddenly felt hot all over. She tore her gaze from his, but it was too late. Already, her heart was racing.

She felt flushed and couldn't believe what had just happened. Shaken, she told Stan from over her shoulder to take charge of entertaining the kids and went inside her house for a moment.

She just wished that Ross would get here. Where was he, anyway? He'd said that he would come. Surely her apology to him over the telephone earlier that week had meant something to him—at least enough for him to want to be here for Jorgie's birthday. Suddenly, Jan appeared in her doorway. "You've got to come out here and see this. He's hilarious."

"Who's hilarious?" Rachel asked.

"Never mind. Just come here," her sister insisted.

Rachel went outside and stood at the end of the patio with her sister.

The children had gathered together and were all sitting down on the ground. In front of them was the clown.

And it didn't take Rachel very long before she was joining in the children's laughter. The clown was a complete klutz. He couldn't juggle, or do magic tricks. He couldn't even get the sunflower he had pinned to his lapel to squirt water at the kids like it was supposed to. Instead he got himself all wet. The kids loved him, though, in spite of his clumsiness, and, in truth, that was something about him that was very appealing.

But Rachel wasn't in any mood for laughing anymore. She was wrestling with the fear that maybe Ross wasn't coming to the party, after all. Maybe he was actually planning to see the kids at some other time, when she wouldn't have to be there with them. The idea made her feel sick inside.

Rachel walked to a secluded area of her backyard. There she drew in a deep breath and told herself that, no matter what, she had to keep up her courage. She just had to. Heaven help her, but it looked as though she would need every ounce of it in the days...months...years to come. It would be a long, lonely life without Ross by her side. But she had no one to blame for that but herself. When he'd wanted to make up for his past mistakes, she'd practically turned her back on him. Now, he was doing the same to her.

Tears stung Rachel's eyes. She glanced back over her shoulder and saw Jan standing nearby, talking to one of the neighborhood children. "Jan," she said, "can you handle the party by yourself for a moment? I need a breath of fresh air."

Her sister looked up at her and frowned. "Yeah—sure. But are you all right?"

"Yes. I'm just a little woozy on my feet. It's the heat, I guess."

Jan's frown deepened. "Honey, don't work yourself into a tizzy. He'll be here. I'm sure of it."

Rachel stiffened. "I know what you're trying to imply, but this has nothing to do with Ross," Rachel replied.

Her sister gave a small laugh. "You can't fool me, big sister. Everything in your life these days is about Ross, and you and I both know it."

Rachel threw up her hands in frustration. It was pointless of her to try to live a lie. Everyone, it seemed, could see right through it. "I'll be back in a minute," she said to Jan before pivoting on her heels and rushing out the side gate. She didn't stop walking until she reached the front corner of her house. Taking another deep breath, she glanced up at the cloudless blue sky and wished with all her heart that she could stop hurting so much inside.

"Rachel?"

Her aching heart froze.

"Rachel, turn around and look at me."

The deep, familiar voice had come from somewhere behind her.

With her pulses racing at an all-time high, Rachel whirled around, expecting to see Ross standing there. But instead, her expectant moment was shattered when she saw it was only the clown she'd hired for Jorgie's birthday. Obviously, she had wanted the voice she had heard to belong to Ross so badly, that she'd actually imagined that it had. Only now she knew better.

Rachel wiped away the few tears that had streaked down her cheeks and attempted a smile. "I'm sorry if you thought I was leaving the party for some reason without paying you first. Wait here. I'll go inside now and get my checkbook. It won't take me but a moment."

With her eyes lowered to the ground, Rachel marched right past the clown and was halfway expecting him to toot his horn at her as he had done earlier. But he didn't. Instead, he said her name.

And once again, she froze.

Then, after a long bewildered moment, she slowly turned around.

And there, standing in the very same spot where the clown had been just moments ago, wearing a clown costume with red punch spilled down the front of it, was Ross. In one of his hands was an orange wig, and in the other was a white cloth that he'd used to wipe off the clown makeup from his face. Stunned, Rachel could only blink at him.

He grinned. "Hi, kitten. Guess I had you fooled, huh?" He began to step out of the costume and that's when Rachel saw he was wearing a pair of blue jeans and a white pullover shirt beneath it.

Still, what she saw happening before her eyes at the moment wasn't making any sense, and she gaped at Ross the whole time he went about the struggling task of removing the clown suit.

Eventually reality began to set in and she started to tremble with pure joy. She had absolutely no idea why Ross had chosen to come to Jorgie's birthday party pretending to be the clown she'd hired for the entertainment, but it didn't really matter. What did matter was the wonderful feeling she had in knowing that he was here—had been here with them all along. *Ross had come, just like he said he would*. And now Rachel knew that somehow, some way, everything was going to be okay for them. It was something in the way Ross was looking at her, she supposed, that made her feel that way. His eyes held tenderness ... need ... and forgiveness. It accelerated her already pounding heart, and she felt like throwing herself into his strong arms.

Instead she continued to smile at him. "Why did you do this?" she asked.

"To make a point."

"You really go out of your way when making a point, don't you," she said.

"So I've been told," he said, and her heart began to palpitate again at just the mere sound of his voice.

He walked up and put his arms around her waist. "How's our love child doing?"

"Love child?"

"Well," he drawled, smiling, "we weren't exactly living together as man and wife when you conceived her, now were we?"

"Her?"

"Oh, didn't I tell you? I put in an order with the Big Man upstairs. I told Him we needed to have a girl and I promised Him that I would be there for you every step of the way. I won't make the same mistake I did a year ago, Rachel."

"I believe you," she said.

He smiled. "And you know what else?"

"No. What?"

By now Ross had a certain sparkle in his eyes. One that Rachel knew right off she would never get tired of seeing.

"Well," he said, "I had someone tell me once that the easiest way to get over being hurt by the one you love, is to let that person kiss your pain away."

"Oh, yeah?" Rachel replied, and a warm glow began to seep through her.

"Yeah," he said with a slow shake of his head. "So, I was wondering, would you like to give it a try?"

Rachel's eyes filled with tears. "Oh, Ross, yes. In a heartbeat."

He cupped the sides of her face in his hands and then he brought his lips down on hers in the sweetest, the most tender kiss he'd ever given her. Then he pulled back just enough to gaze into her eyes. "How do you feel now? All better?"

"Mmm...wonderful," she said. "And you?"

For just a moment he searched her eyes as a smile tilted up the corners of his mouth. "Healed, my love. All healed."

"I love you, Ross Murdock."

"I love you, too, Rachel Murdock."

And then he took her lips again.

Suddenly someone cleared her voice behind them. "Okay, okay, you two, let's break it up," her sister said. "The kids are all watching through the crack in the fence—and you know the notorious reputation you already have around here. Anyway, I don't think the neighborhood parents are going to appreciate the idea of you teaching their little darlings about the birds and the bees. This is a birthday party, for heaven's sake."

When Ross and Rachel broke apart and looked at her in a startled daze, she laughed. "Just kidding, guys. Just kidding." Then she moved in closer and said, "But, just to be on the safe side, keep it G-rated, will you?"

Looking at each other, Ross and Rachel smiled. Then they turned together toward the sounds of their children's laughter.

And in that moment Rachel was so happy she felt she might burst open with joy. Now she was able to look to the future and know that she and her children were going to be where they belonged.

And Ross. Never in her wildest dreams could she have imagined him as the husband and father he had become. He was ready now to give of himself to his family, and, in truth, that was all she'd ever wanted of him.

In fact, it was easy for anyone to see that the Murdock family was richer today by far. At last, they had found something money couldn't buy them.

They had found each other.

And love. Lots and lots of love.

Epilogue

Eight months later

"Yessiree, it's a girl, all right," Rachel's obstetrician said as he lifted up the squalling newborn and placed her on her mother's stomach while he cut the umbilical cord. "A fine, healthy baby girl. What are you going to name her?"

"Amy Nicole," Rachel replied through her tears. She sounded exhausted, but to Ross, her serene expression was as radiant as the early morning sunrise on a cloudless day.

He had been at Rachel's side throughout her labor, coaching her and doing his best to make her as comfortable as possible. Now, as tears gathered in his eyes, too, he squeezed her hand reassuringly so she would know that he was proud of her. Then he bent and kissed her tenderly on the lips.

Her eyes lifted. "Oh, Ross, I couldn't have done it without you."

Ross gazed deeply into her eyes. "Sweetheart, I wouldn't have missed sharing this moment with you for the world."

Within moments their daughter was ready to be held and Ross stepped aside momentarily so that the nurse could place her in Rachel's arms. He watched in awe, his heart thumping with excitement. It was a priceless moment for him, symbolic in so many ways of all he'd almost lost.

After a while, Rachel lifted her eyes from their newborn daughter's face. Ross smiled at her, his heart swelling with pride.

"I love you, Rachel," he said, "more than anything in the whole world."

"I love you, too, Ross," she replied.

He bent and kissed their newborn daughter's petal-soft forehead. "She's beautiful," he said, "just like her mother." Then he kissed Rachel again, just because he needed to. "When will the boys be able to see her? I know that they're anxious. And, undoubtedly, Jan is too. They're all waiting outside."

Rachel smiled, her eyes shining with joy. "Probably as soon as I'm taken back to my room, a nurse will bring her to us so we can all be together as a family."

A family. He wondered if Rachel truly understood what she and his children meant to him. He had a feeling she did, though. Lord knew, he told her so at every opportunity.

He was at peace now with himself and the security that had once eluded him had since nestled in all around him in the form of Rachel's gentle, loving

smile. She was his anchor…his foundation…his heart
and soul.

In all the ways that really mattered, Ross Murdock
truly thought himself among the wealthiest of men.

He was, indeed, a very lucky man.

*   *   *   *   *